"Don't let Andrew Dice Clay prevent you from reading this. Substitute J. J. Gittes and you'll have a great ride. From coast to coast Ford Fairlane knows his way around the scene. With Tom Waits–like prose, you'll be out-hipped. Rex Weiner is so hip."

—**John Densmore**, The Doors

"Fast-paced, engaging storytelling. Pure adrenaline! If Philip Marlowe was reincarnated as a punk rock PI navigating the devastated war zone of downtown Manhattan in the late seventies, he would look a lot like Rex Weiner's unforgettable Ford Fairlane."

—**Jonathan Shaw**, author of *Narcisa: Our Lady of Ashes* and *Scab Vendor: Confessions of a Tattoo Artist*

"The resurrected Ford Fairlane stories are a breezy, joyously perverse, laugh-out-loud pleasure: part Chandler, part Philip K. Dick—and all Rex Weiner."

—**Bruce Wagner**, author of *Dead Stars* and *I Met Someone*

"If you miss the New York City that was edgy, messy, filthy, after-hours, and off-the-books—you know, the city with a rock and roll heart—please welcome back Ford Fairlane."

—**Joe Nick Patoski**, author of *Stevie Ray Vaughan: Caught in the Crossfire* and *Willie Nelson: An Epic Life*; host of the Texas Music Hour of Power, Marfa Public Radio

The (Original) Adventures of

Ford Fairlane

The Long-Lost Rock 'n' Roll Detective Stories

The (Original) Adventures of

Ford Fairlane

The Long-Lost Rock 'n' Roll Detective Stories

REX WEINER

A Vireo Book | Rare Bird Books
Los Angeles, Calif.

A Vireo Book | Rare Bird Books
453 South Spring Street, Suite 302
Los Angeles, CA 90013
rarebirdbooks.com

Copyright © 2018 by Rex Weiner

FIRST TRADE PAPERBACK ORIGINAL EDITION

Set in Warnock Pro
Printed in the United States

10 9 8 7 6 5 4 3 2 1

Publisher's Cataloging-in-Publication data
available upon request.

Dedicated to Carlos Laszlo

"Break on through to the other side..."

—The Doors

Contents

How The Adventures of
Ford Fairlane were Created

PEOPLE ALWAYS ASK ME how much of my original stories made it into the movie, and I have to say it's all there in the stories. And there's more where that came from…much more.

It all began when I was living in a Manhattan loft on Twenty-Second Street between Fifth and Sixth avenues—what the real-estate wheels now call the Flatiron District. Back then, in the 1970s, it was just another sooty warehouse side street with trucks unloading noisily. My building—six floors of copper-wire coils, fluorescent light fixtures, circuit breakers, and other crap was owned by an electrician who made all his bucks in the 1950s and '60s wiring the exploding post-war school system in city suburbs. Now the Baby Boomers were hipsters like me looking for raw loft space, and with no more fat municipal contracts to fill his coffers Mr. Electric was ready to turn out the lights and retire to Florida.

My girlfriend, Deanne Stillman, and I bought the place, fixed it up a little, and had a blast. We were writing for magazines, publishing books, running something called the Underground Press Syndicate, making a bit of money, and keeping a fifty pound tank of nitrous oxide in the corner just for laughs, so to speak. Our social circle included the dopers at *High Times*, where I was a member of the founding editorial staff, and the first cast of *Saturday Night Live*, due to the fact that Deanne was best buddies with *SNL* writer Anne Beatts and Judy Jacklin, consorts of Michael O'Donoghue and John Belushi, respectively.

Our regular watering hole was The Bells of Hell on Thirteenth Street, where some of the National Lampoon crowd—Doug Kenney, Ted Mann, Tony Hendra, etc.—came to get liquored up and snort lines of blow off the bar after last call. The Bells was also home to crusty journalists from the *Daily News*, the *New York Post*, and *The Village Voice*, along with a chorus of bibulous writers drawn from the rock-crit ranks including Lester Bangs, Nick Tosches, Billy Altman, and John Morthland.

Occasionally, I'd get up onstage in The Bells back room with my rock group, King Rude, opening for Turner & Kirwan of Wexford, the Irish house band (it was, after all, an Irish bar). We did mostly covers of obscure blues tunes and a few original rocking ditties penned by guitar slinger and Screw columnist Joe Kane ("Smut From The Past") and myself, songs with titles like "I'm Pissed Off At

You," and "Coma Baby." Occasionally, the great East Village Other writer Dean Latimer would get up and sing his classic "California Sunshine Girl," a hilarious epic about a Midwest guy who follows his sweet little hometown girlfriend out to Hollywood only to discover her performing onscreen in a hardcore-porn flick, with the various acts yodeled by Dean in scabrous detail.

Our drummer was Don Cristensen who also played with the legendary Contortions. They were part of the so-called No Wave scene, a raucous rejoinder to the new wave scene, which was itself a rebuke to the punk rock scene, much of which revolved around the infamous CBGB on the Bowery. King Rude, in its original incarnation as Blind Orange Julius, was one of the first bands that CBGB owner Hilly Kristal booked to play his joint under the impression that we were a blues band, essential to Hilly's quirky vision of a club featuring Country, Blue Grass, and Blues music.

Actually, we could barely play worth shit and had no equipment. Our first gig, on a double bill with a band we ridiculed for its stupid name, the Ramones, we just plugged our guitars into the amps that were sitting idly by. The Ramones returned in person and took issue with our use of their equipment. During the ensuing argument, I slipped a few bucks to a henchman who went to a local bakery and returned with a meringue pie that I heaved into Joey Ramone's face. That effectively ended Blind Orange Julius's engagement at CBGB.

Don, the drummer, invited me to check out his other gigs, and I began heading out after dark to late-night downtown joints like Tier 3, Mudd Club, Club 57, and various lofts and cellars where the late-seventies music was happening.

To be honest, I had lost my taste for music ever since it turned into the "music industry" in the modern sense. I could never sit in a stadium watching rockers "rock." And when disco overran R&B, it seemed to obliterate the place where the music began, which was the blues. If I couldn't hear a backbeat, I didn't want to hear it at all.

But there was something happening in those late-night clubs that intrigued me—a lifestyle, a scene, a discordant rejection of the music industry, lots of heroin and too much alcohol, and more than a hint of violence in the air. New York was a dangerous place in those days.

I decided I wanted to write about it all, but I was tired of the journalistic pose. I didn't want to "report" on things anymore, and I certainly didn't care to issue critiques on the music—for bands I liked or didn't like. That seemed pointless. What I liked was the texture and *language* of the scene— bands with names like Teenage Jesus and the Jerks, Defunkt, The Raybeats; self-invented characters like Lydia Lunch and the music, described by one critic venturing forth with "the most ferociously avant-garde and aggressively ugly music since Albert Ayler puked all over my brain back in— what?—sixty-four."

So I invented a character loosely modeled on myself, a streetwise young dude, armed with a knowledge of music history that helped him do the job he had to do: chasing down secrets, the mysteries of the music. He was a private eye, a detective in the classic film noir mode, a "new wave detective" (as the first stories were originally subtitled) who worked in the music business, a man who knew everybody and everybody knew him. He was professional, dedicated, and he had style, but was ready to tangle with anybody who tried to cross him. And you wouldn't want to cross Ford Fairlane.

In some ways, the writing was a literary experiment: how to make a fictional character real by surrounding him with real people and real places. Off the top of my head (with echoes of Ford Madox Ford, for some reason), I gave my hero the name Ford Fairlane. It sounded like rock and roll.

In other ways, my experiment was also an attempt to escape a rut. My relationship was falling apart, my patience with a post-Watergate journalistic writing career wearing thin. I'd always imagined myself a New York City writer living in the world of writing, editing, and publishing. I'd been a publisher at the age of twenty-one (*The New York Ace*) and had my first Op-Ed piece in *The New York Times* at twenty-two. My exploits in the radical politico "underground" scene had already been chronicled in the *Times* and *New York* magazine, and my nonfiction book, *The Woodstock Census: Nationwide Survey of the Sixties Generation*, coauthored with Deanne, had been published to good reviews by Viking, along with a five-city tour. But after nearly a decade, none of it seemed to add up to anything. Where was I destined to find my ultimate niche—*The New York Review of Books*? Highly unlikely.

The first Ford Fairlane "adventure" was published in the now-defunct *New York Rocker* in 1979, a ragged little black-and-white newsprintzine. Andy Schwartz, the nerdy music fanboy who was publisher/editor, agreed—amiably enough but without a great deal of enthusiasm—to serialize my story in six biweekly installments. I wrote them fast and dirty, not knowing where the plot would lead, using whatever I encountered by day or night in the streets and clubs. And the deal was, I was writing for free. Not that I couldn't have used the money. At some point I'd moved out of the loft to a basement hole in the Chelsea Hotel and from there to a cold-water dump on First and First, just off Houston Street, with a hole in the floor where junkies had blown through and jumped down to rob the candy store below. The Ford Fairlane stories were typed out with gloves on, with an empty belly and a head full of Old Overholt whisky while puffing packs of Camels, unfiltered. In those days, I was sad, mad, and bad. Ford was my outlet for all my dark, violent, and discordant feelings, which was the tenor of the times in late 1970s Gotham, a bankrupt municipality that even the president of the United States advised to "drop dead." As Ford Fairlane says, "It's a dangerous decade, baby."

California was far away. Too much sunshine always seemed like a clever lie to a New Yorker like me. Never in my days on the city's mean streets, from where I was born in 1950s Brooklyn to my 1960s days on the Lower East Side to my last stint in Hell's Kitchen toward the tail end of the 1970s, did I imagine I'd end up in California, much less in Hollywood making movies and TV. Blame it all on Ford Fairlane.

My break came when my old friend Paul Krassner, yippie jester behind the groundbreaking satirical journal *The Realist*, got a gig in October 1980 as head writer for something called *The Steve Allen Election Eve Comedy Special* for a new cable TV company called HBO. It was the dawn of the Reagan Era, and Krassner hired me to come out to Hollywood and join the writing staff. I'd never written for television before. But the money was decent, and what the hell: it seemed like a nice break from the dreariness on First and First, where my professional poker player roommate Shay Addams (down on his luck after being banned from Vegas casinos due to his proficiency at card counting) and I were breaking up furniture to burn in the fireplace for heat. And if

The (Original) Adventures of Ford Fairlane

I could stick it to right-winger Ronnie Reagan with some sharp jokes, that would be just dandy.

Staying at the Magic Motel on Franklin, just under the Hollywood Hills, I called my old pal Richard Meltzer, one of the original rock crits, and he took me to see Darby Crash at the Starwood. Meltzer introduced me to the LA punk scene, totally different from New York's but no less compelling, and I started hanging out at the Zero Zero, Rajis, The Masque, and other dumps around town. My friend Jay Levin, formerly of the *New York Post*, had founded the *LA Weekly*, and as publisher he agreed to publish a second Ford Fairlane adventure for the *Weekly*, this one bringing my rock and roll PI to LA in the same Dickensian serialization as the first one.

In between writing sessions at HBO's brand-new offices high atop Century City's South Tower (none of my jokes and few of Krassner's made it into the show), I was hanging in the clubs, getting laid, doing whatever pills and powders came my way, and turning in the Ford Fairlane stories. Like New York in the first adventure, the City of Angels became a character in the second series of episodes. That time and place of dive bars and funky pre-foodie restaurants, most of which no longer exist, was captured in one sentence describing a day in Ford Fairlane's LA life: "Lunch at Duke's. Pinball at Barney's Beanery. A steak dinner at Port's. Booze and nine-ball at the Raincheck." I had no idea if anybody liked the stories, but had some fun writing them. When the HBO gig was finished and I left LA for New York, I had no idea what was in store for Ford, or for me. *Maybe*, I thought, *some smart editor at a publishing house will pick it up as a detective series.* Or something.

As luck would have it, I got a job as editor of *Swank*, "The Magazine for Men," one of many *Playboy* knockoffs launched in the 1950s. Mario Puzo and Bruce Jay Friedman were among my predecessors, once publishing fiction by the likes of Norman Mailer, Graham Greene, and Arthur C. Clarke. I would be the last editor when there were still articles to edit (they went to an all-photo format after I departed). Editing a girly mag was a snap. It lifted me out of the ranks of starving journos and into the executive suite. My office on Fifty-Seventh and Seventh overlooked Carnegie Hall. If I left my window open to the early spring breezes I could hear Frank Sinatra rehearsing for his comeback concert while the day's aspiring centerfold stripped in front of my desk.

New York was starting to look like it had possibilities again. Each evening I would walk home from work across Times Square to my pad in Hell's Kitchen, stopping at joints along the way like Bernard's and the Melody Burlesque to schmooze with bartenders and strippers, street poets and pill-heads, downtown graffiti artists and uptown culture vultures, and fellow editors and writers aspiring to what Terry Southern called the "quality lit game," thinking everything was the way it was going to be. The great Gotham churn of hopes and dreams, leavened by the recapitulation of daily life, was my future present.

Then one day I got a phone call from somebody who said he was a movie producer. He said he'd read my Ford Fairlane stories in *LA Weekly* and he thought they'd make a good movie. Was I interested? I hung up on the guy, convinced it was one of my drinking buddies pulling a prank.

Six months later, in October 1981, I was in Hollywood under contract to Columbia Pictures to write the screenplay for a movie based on my Ford Fairlane stories. I had my name on a parking space at the studio (located then in Burbank), an office, a secretary, and a fat per diem that allowed me a room at the Chateau Marmont and a vintage Mustang convertible from Rent-a-Wreck, not to mention all the trouble that cash money can buy.

The producer was Floyd Mutrux (*Freebie and the Bean, Dusty and Sweets McGee*) who was also proposing to direct. A funny little dude with a scruffy beard and complicated private life involving several ex-wives, kids, girlfriends, the whole Hollywood schmear, Floyd had a rock and roll sensibility, along with a Ferrari, a vintage Mercedes, inhabiting a world of substance abuse and young babes. All of which he proceeded to share with me during the year we spent running all over LA writing the script.

It was never clear to me if he understood my stories, or if he'd ever even read them. Floyd had his own particular take on Ford Fairlane that was more a kind of mood than an actual story or character that he struggled to impart to me. Sometimes, rocketing along Mulholland at midnight in his top-down Ferrari with X blasting from the Bose speakers and the city lights twinkling down below, I'd think: *Yeah, now I get it.* But most of the time we were just raising hell from one end of LA to the other. At least he was teaching me screenplay writing as we went along; Floyd was a savvy instructor and I learned a lot—when we were both sober. I learned that screenwrititng is tough, Although a lot of fools out there are trying, you really have to be a good writer, first of all. Then you must learn what goes on in front of and behind the camera, not to mention what goes on inside the fickle head of a studio executive. In any case, I got pretty good at it—good enough to sell a few scripts, and even teach screenwriting classes in later years. But back then I hadn't a clue. I figured I'd polish off the damn screenplay, collect the check, quit this crazy Hollywood ride, and head back to New York.

In the end, Columbia was sold by its owners, Coca Cola, to the Japanese, becoming Sony Entertainment. Lost in the translation, Ford Fairlane went into a kind of limbo called turnaround. Nearly every studio in town had a swing at it, each time optioning my original stories—since my smart agent had managed for me to retain the rights to my original material—and then commissioning a screenplay. Along the way, over the years, I joined the Writers Guild and became one of the first writers hired to create the TV series *Miami Vice*. Keeping my hand in journalism, several articles were optioned and one made into the Turner Network's first made-for-TV movie (*Forgotten Prisoners: The Amnesty Files*). I got married, had a kid, bought a house, acquired a hacienda in Mexico, and sold the New York loft, closing off that part of my life. It seemed I was in California to stay, all due to Ford Fairlane—which took a helluva of a long time to get onto the big screen.

When the producer Joel Silver (*Die Hard*) finally came to me in 1988 and said he wanted to make my stories into a movie, I said sure. My agent made the deal, I turned in a whole new screenplay, did revisions, and other writers came aboard. Andrew Dice Clay, the hot, young comic star at the time, was cast in the leading role. Renny Harlin was given the directing job—not because an action director from Helsinki knows the first thing about directing a Jewish stand-up comic from Brooklyn—but as a prerequisite for directing *Die Hard 2*. Daniel Waters (*Heathers*) did a final polish on the screenplay.

So, finally, cameras began rolling on *The Adventures of Ford Fairlane*, nearly ten years from when I'd first started writing the stories that are collected here, for the first time, in their original form. Whatever made it onto the big screen from these stories, or from my original screenplay, can be debated, but that's besides the point. The movie got made, I got paid, and that's that. My feature film credit as arbitrated by the Writers Guild (in the days before the rule that first screenplay writer always gets a writing credit) was "Based on characters created by Rex Weiner." Fair enough, I guess.

One day during filming I got a call from "The Diceman" requesting that I come visit the set; he wanted to work up some new jokes with the original writer. We sat around the trailer and had some laughs. Then suddenly he got up and said, "C'mon with me a sec." We go outside where the crew is setting up the lights and moving the camera for the next shot. Dice says, "Hey! Everybody, lissen up! This here's Rex Weiner, the writer. He's the reason we all got jobs, okay?"

The crew all looked at Dice like he was the biggest shmuck and then went back to their work. I went back to my life knowing that although it's not every day that you get an idea in your head and it turns into a Hollywood movie, it's not that big of a deal.

On the other hand, these stories—which at their best, in short, dirty strokes and minimalistic style, capture a time and place we'll never see again—did change my life.

Thanks, Ford!

NEW YORK

Chapter 1

Where it all began

THE LIGHTS GLIMMERED DOWN Broadway like a strand of pearls slung over a black girl's thigh. Bleecker Street flashed by, then Houston. The windshield wipers beat rhythm to the cabbie's dull monologue. "Quit the chatter," I told him, "and step on it."

"Two ay em and the fella's in a hurry," the cabbie groused.

Damn right. My rush hour starts when everyone else's ends. Long after the nine-to-fivers have switched off Carson and sunk into dreamland, that's when I'm getting into high gear. Sure, I work weird hours. Some people say *I'm* weird. But nobody says I don't take care of business. Tonight I was taking care of business. And while traffic lights on Broadway flipped green, a pale light in my brain kept flashing *Caution! Caution!* For comfort, I patted my coat beneath my left shoulder: the .44 was there, ready.

The taxi skidded around the corner of Walker Street. I got out. The usual crowd stood outside the

Mudd Club, looking like jerks and yammering to be let in. I elbowed my way though and Richie ushered me in the door.

"Glad you're here," he said. "Ike's upstairs. He's been causing trouble all night."

I ran into Jane Jelly, singer for the Slithereens, coming down the stairs. I used to know her as Jane Blatzky before she found out she could sing like a banshee and be hailed as a pop star. It helped that she had a body like Jayne Mansfield. I asked her if she'd seen Ike. Jane pointed upstairs.

"He's totally out of control. Completely maxed. Somebody should do something about him." She smiled at me. "Speaking of doing something, what're you doing later, Ford?"

I might have had a good time that night if not for that cretin named Ike. I took a rain check with Jane and continued up to the club's inner sanctum.

The place was jammed tight: pop stars, cheap filmmakers, a couple of Ramones, two Dead Boys, a Helmut Newton–model looking icy, assorted sycophants, art students, and trendies. Just a lot of mouths flapping in the breeze. Ike was there, too.

Ike Schmidt was the lead singer for the Argumentative Types. It was one of those computer bands from Germany, the kind that made music like the sound effects you hear in old sci-fi movies. He was standing in the corner, talking too loud and weeping at the same time. A real mess. My guess was 'ludes and red wine. That's a bad mix. Everyone knows 'ludes go only with white.

The club owner, a thin, nervous guy with a Long Island accent named Steve, was trying to talk the slob into leaving. When Steve spotted me, he looked relieved.

"You know Ford Fairlane," he soothed Ike. "He's a detective. He'll protect you, Ike. Now won't you go outside?"

"But they'll kill me! They'll kill me, I tell you!"

I told Ike to shut his mouth and took him by the arm. He wouldn't stop blubbering. He was a big guy with a nasty streak and a rep for beating up on audiences. It was part of the band's mystique. But now Ike let me lead him downstairs and out the door like a baby. After going a few yards down Walker Street, I steered him into an alley. Then I slammed the creep against the brick wall.

"Vat you vant?" he whined piteously.

I ran it down quickly and plainly. My client, a very famous rock and roller, was missing his favorite guitar. It was a Link Wray lyre-body Danelectro, one of only five ever made. Ike Schmidt was the last one seen with the rare axe. I'd been hired to retrieve it.

"Dat's a lie," Ike spat. "I neffer took dat guitar."

He seemed scared. Too scared. I wondered why. This game had to be played carefully, or else he might light up "tilt."

"Where is it, Ike? Maybe this is all a big mistake."

"She gave it to me."

"Who?"

"Vait a minute, I tell you."

I waited while Ike fumbled in his coat pocket. If it was a knife, my left arm was flexed from shoulder to pinky, my right leg poised to kick his wrist into another time zone. Instead, he came up with a tiny bit of folded paper and unwrapped it. Nose candy.

"Vant some?" he smiled thinly. "Iss goot shit."

"You first," I said, and watched him take a snort. I don't mind a snort now and then, especially when I'm partying. But this wasn't my idea of a party.

"Dis girl," sniffed Ike, "she got the guitar. Also, she giff me dis coke. Ah!"

He rubbed his charred nostrils with his bony fingers. The tips were thick with callouses from playing guitar. I asked him what the girl's name was.

"Shirley. From Cincinnati. Got fantastic hair, cut like a Mohawk, you know? It is dyed red und white und blue. I met her here one night und she came to my room bringing dis guitar. I didn't know nothing about it. Then last Friday she took the guitar back and she...HAUGHHH!"

Ike suddenly grabbed his throat and went down, eyes pooping out of his head like a couple of overdone Brussels sprouts. His faced turned purple and he clawed at the air.

"Help!" he gasped. "Help me!"

I couldn't do shit for the poor sick bastard and that's the fucking truth. How do I know? Because

I took what was let of the white powder to the lab the next day and got a report.

It was 99 percent pure Drano.

My guess was that somebody, possibly named Shirley, was out to shut the German's fat mouth. They'd done a pretty good job of it, too. Not only did I have to let him croak in that alley off Walker Street, but now the word was out that the last guy seen with the stiff was Ford Fairlane. I had exactly one chance to exit this bad scene and I chanced it the next night.

"S'matter, Ford, stickup the Chase Manhattan?" said Jack, holding open the door for me at Hurrah. "The cops was here. Dey was axing 'bout you."

I knew they would be. The fuzz knew I used to do security at this club, among a score of others, before I got sick of it and went for my PI license. I'd taught Jack, a former Bed-Stuy Golden Gloves champ, everything he knew about being a door bouncer, including a memory trick for recalling names together with faces. Now I was counting on him to be an A student. I asked him what he knew about a gal named Shirley.

"Chick name of Shirley? With a Mohawk? Lemme think, now. She have a red, white, and blue dye job? She from Cincinnati? Yeah, sure I know her. Used to come here all the time. Real heavy into Dead Boys, Pere Ubu—all those Ohio groups."

"Seen her lately? Know when she might be back around?"

"Forget it, man. She won't be back nowheres. Didn't you read about it in the papers? She went back to Cincinnati and scored free tickets to a Who concert. I hear Shirley was first on line when the crowd broke loose. Lotta folks got stepped on and snuffed."

Shit! My one goddamned alibi, trampled to death.

"Funny thing is," said Jack, "she didn't even like The Who. She just dug being first on line, know what I mean?"

I needed to think and think fast. Shooting a few games of pinball at Playland in Times Square helped clear my head. I was being framed for murder in somebody's dirty game. Somewhere, a dirty rat held the rule book and I had to find him—or her. But first I had to get some shuteye. So just as dawn crawled up over the East River, I slipped up the back way to my flat on St. Marks Place. A peek through the blinds told me what I'd suspected: two plainclothesmen were staked out across the way, dressed like bums. But bums don't have new heels on their shoes.

I fell into bed and was out like a light. Maybe I'd wake up in jail, but I was too tired to care. Then the phone jangled and I picked it up with only half my brain functioning. It was a girl's voice. She said her name was Shirley, she had something important to tell me about a guitar, and I should meet her at Tier 3 tonight. At the same awful moment, somebody was beating my door down, shouting "Police! Police!" It wasn't the rock band, either.

Chapter 2

Laffs and stilettos on the Lower East Side

SOME SMART ALECK INVENTED a tool they call "The Claw." Cops use it to rip doors down. The Claw was doing a Godzilla act on mine. I could hear the cops swearing out in the hallway. Three heavy-duty dead-bolt locks stood between them and me. The first one popped off the frame and shot clear across the room.

I threw on some fresh threads and tucked my shooter under my arm. There was a switch behind a bookcase. I flicked it. A wall panel fell back. The second door lock clattered to the floor. I crammed inside the dusty dumbwaiter and the wall panel slid shut. This getaway gizmo was something I'd inherited from the previous tenant, a sixties radical–type with a fondness for mixing black powder and national monuments. I hear he's still loose and I wish the bastard a lot of luck.

The dumbwaiter got me to the basement that led to an alleyway that led to fresh air, sunshine, and Second Avenue. While the boys in blue were frisking my pad, I was ordering breakfast at the B&H

luncheonette. Max, the counterman, served me a plate of French toast and a face full of scowl.

"Yer a popular guy today, ain'tcha?" Max said to me.

"Quit spitting when you talk, Max."

"Wise guy. First the cops come askin' fer ya this mornin', now this shmegegge over here."

"Over where?" I asked, not turning my head.

"S'funny," said Max. "The guy was sittin' there a minute ago. You walked in and he was sittin' right over there havin' coffee and babka."

"What'd he look like?"

"No nose."

"Quit pulling my yo-yo, Max, this is life and death."

"I swear, this guy had no nose in his face, just a big sorta hole in the middle. A skinny guy with no beak and he looked like trouble. Like you, shmuck, always lookin' for trouble."

"Don't spit in my food, Max."

The record store outside was blaring out "Hunted" by The Passions. I lamped the street for cops and found myself lucky. Stepping sideways to the newsstand at Gem Spa, I dropped a quarter on the rubber mat and picked up a *Post*. Someone leaned over my shoulder. His breath could have stripped paint.

"Looth jointh?"

He had a wool cap pulled low, wrap-around mirrored shades, a shabby overcoat, and a harelip.

Forget it, I said, and moved to go. He blocked my way and smiled dreamily. In his hand was a K55, a cheap gravity knife that can perform expensive surgery.

"Leth walk," he said.

We walked. I told the slimeball we didn't need to travel, he could have my wallet right there on Second Avenue. He only laughed and dug the steel point into my lower lumbar region.

"I'm takin' ya to Thpinkth. He wanth to thee ya."

"Spinks? You mean the boxer?"

"Don't be funny, thonny. I thaid Thpinkth. Wid an eff."

He shoved me around the corner onto Seventh Street. I said I didn't get it. Could he explain that again?

"Eff, eff. Ya know, Thpinkth. Ya heard me."

Couldn't figure it out. The harelip had me halfway down the deserted block. I had to think fast, double-talking him in the meantime.

"Eff? As in Fred? Eff as in ferry, eff as in fire, eff as in…" The newspaper fell accidentally on purpose from my hand. It distracted him long enough for me to whip around, catch his Adam's apple in a yubi-waza punch, and drop him in a writhing heap on the asphalt. I'm sure it didn't do his speech impediment any good.

"Eff as in fuck you."

Midnight found me chugging a Bud at the Tier 3 bar. I was looking for Shirley, hoping she'd take me off the cops' wanted list, and still wondering what the harelip had been trying to tell me. A combo called the Raybeats was capping a set. I scanned the rockers and marked a lot of hairdos: beehives, flips, flattops, razor cuts, and skinheads. But no Mohawks, no Shirley. The Raybeats performed "Green Onions," then took a break.

The drummer, a character named Don, parked himself next to me at the bar. He's got the kind of face that looks at home under a pork pie hat. The guitar player named Jody sat down too. I gave them a rundown of my blind date. They hadn't seen her.

"Working on another case," asked Don, "or just having fun?"

"Don't know yet," I said, and worked the talk around the missing Danelectro. "A Link Wray lyre–body?" said Jody. "There's only five of those ever made."

Don said it was a funny thing because two musicians he knew were also missing guitars. "A fifty-nine Gibson Sunburst Les Paul, and the other guy had an ES three-three-five Gibson Dotmarker, nineteen sixty."

"And there was that guy I read about," said Jody. "He owned Jimi Hendrix's powder-blue Fender Strat with the maple neck and it got ripped off."

A rash of guitar heists, all of them rare models: I put the figures in a column but I didn't get a chance to add them up. My calculator jammed at the sight of a red, white, and blue Mohawk and a long pair of legs gliding up the stairs. I left my pals at the bar.

The upstairs room is always dark, except for the colored strobes that flash on faces. I tried to pick her out. The shadows held a menagerie of 'lude freaks, gropers, reggae rudies, beatnoids, and brooding art students.

"Here," a voice whispered.

She was sitting in the corner. My eyes adjusted to the dark enough to see a pretty face. I could take or leave the shaved skull with the single strip of dyed hair down the middle, but the rest of her had nice geometry. I took a seat.

"You're supposed to be dead in that Who riot."

"This kid's all right," she smiled. "That was just somebody who borrowed my ID for the night. Poor Susie. Oh well, it's only rock and roll."

She was maybe eighteen and smooth as ice cream. I could have eaten her with a spoon. But I had to kick myself hard. She was the one who'd snuffed Ike, a killer in a red-vinyl miniskirt. Still, it was tough to not trust the little sweetheart. I decided to play the thing straight.

"Got any more of that stuff you slipped Ike?"

She looked up with frightened eyes, big enough to swim in.

"That wasn't my fault," she whispered.

"Mine either. That's why I'm taking you downtown."

"I know. They think you killed him. I'll go to the police. I'll tell them everything. That's what you want, isn't it?"

"Sure."

"All right," she said. "I'll do it. For you. But you have to do something for me first."

"No deal."

"Just give me a chance to explain everything to you."

"Shoot."

"Not here."

"Where?"

"Do you want to see the Danelectro?"

"Let's go."

We split the club. She said the hot axe was stashed in her loft up the street. Walking on West Broadway, I felt the wind razor the back of my neck. Hell no, I wasn't going to follow Shirley into that loft, no way. I figured it for a setup. But my idea was to peep the address first, then drag her downtown to play canary. That way the cops could take care of their case and I could take care of mine. I had it all figured out.

Hound-dog cabs streaked uptown looking for fares. Overhead, a jet snarled looking for a place to land. A street cleaner sucked the gutter. A dead *Daily News* blew by, followed by a bum in a wool cap pulled low and a shabby overcoat. Then, too late, I heard the words again.

"Looth jointh?"

I went for my piece but the creep sapped me hard. A flash of red vinyl, then there was nothing. Nothing.

Chapter 3

Fifty-Two Pick-up or Die

WHEN I CAME TO I was in a carnival and my head was the Ferris wheel. It finally slowed down enough for me to make out a big loft crammed with electronic equipment. I tried to sit up but my hands were lashed to the cot.

"Relaxth."

The harelip stood over me, grinning. Next to him was a little skinny guy who was missing something: a nose. Suddenly it made sense.

"I'm Sphinx," he said in a voice like Freon. "You have already met my associate, Pointy. I'm sure you can guess how I obtained my own name. But can you guess why Pointy has his?"

"No idea, bub."

"It's easy. Show him, Pointy."

Pointy the hairlip flicked his wrist and the K55 clicked open. He clamped my left hand in his and inserted the cool blade beneath the nail of my little finger.

"You see? He only uses the point."

***

It was a big loft. Maybe twenty by thirty. I could see an elevator. There was a little room off to one side. I counted six columns holding up the ceiling. I counted them to keep my mind off my lacerated digit. It hurt like a motherfucker and I wanted to kill. Except I was tied down and the bastards had me where they wanted me.

"The pain is entirely unnecessary," smirked the guy named Sphinx. "Just tell us what we wish to know."

"What if I don't?"

"My associate will remove each of your remaining fingernails."

"What if I still don't talk?"

Pointy grabbed my ear and made a slicing motion in the air. The van Gogh treatment. That was bad. But I was curious.

"And what if I *still* don't talk?"

Sphinx smiled and turned to his harelipped pal.

"Pointy, why don't you play your favorite record for our guest?"

The place was jammed with all kinds of electronic gear. There were about five synthesizers, three control boards, all kinds of hook-ups, input-outputs, thick spaghetti bundles of wires draped from the ceiling and walls, and a massive phalanx of speakers.

Pointy pressed a button.

A giant boom rotated. It touched a tall stack of records, then slid downward. Then it touched another stack of discs, moving upward. Then it paused. The mechanical claw grasped Pointy's choice. It slid out. The arm rotated. It slung the disc onto the turntable. This monstrous jukebox was equipped with a perfect sound system. Only a genius could have rigged such acoustics: subtle, powerful. The only defect was Pointy's taste: Lou Reed's *Metal Machine Music*. Full volume.

"Okay! Okay! Shut it off, I'll talk!"

Sphinx nodded. Pointy, disappointed, poked the button. The hellish robot switched off. These guys were connoisseurs of torture. I figured I'd better play the game their way for now. But the game—was it five-card stud or fifty-two pickup? Sphinx threw out the first card.

"What did Ike Schmidt tell you before he died?"

I relayed all the details: Shirley, the stolen guitar she laid on Ike, the coke that turned out to be poison.

"What else?"

"Nothing."

"Nothing about...*Martin*?" I shook my head.

"Martin. Martin. The name means nothing to you?"

"Martin makes a good classical guitar."

"Don't be funny! You're hiding something!"

"Fuck off!"

"Pointy..."

The demented harelip, drooling, slid the point of his knife halfway under my thumbnail. If wishes were sulfuric acid, he would have dissolved. But as it was, I sweated. And sucked a lot of spit. Sphinx glanced at his watch.

"We don't have much time. I ask you again, what do you know about Martin?" "I don't know anything!"

"Ike knew too much," he muttered.

A bell rang somewhere. Sphinx looked worried. He snapped his fingers and Pointy put away his blade. I breathed easier.

"Put him in the room and shut him up," he said. "The others are coming. The meeting will finish in two hours. After that, Mr. Fairlane, you'll be given one more chance. Then..."

"Then what?"

Sphinx shrugged. "You die."

I was gagged and packed away in the dark room on the side of the elevator. It was soundproofed, apparently for recording purposes. Lying still, I could barely hear things happening in the loft: the elevator traveling up and down; people walking around; chairs scraping the floor; muffled voices, many of them. And then my eyes grew used to the dark and I saw something unbelievable.

Along the walls of the room hung about forty or fifty guitars. There was a '59 Gibson Sunburst Les Paul; a '58 powder blue Stratocaster with what looked like the original maple neck. I saw a 335 Gibson ES Dotmarker hanging next to an original Gibson Byrdland. And right over my head was the *Link Wray lyre–body Danelectro*. Rare, fantastic guitars were all over the place, all hot merchandise—worth about half a million bucks. But the unbelievable thing was each guitar was frozen forever in a coffin of solid, crystal-clear Plexiglas. Nobody would ever play these guitars again.

No doubt about it. These guys were perverts.

Looking for a way out, I craned my neck, pulling at the cords binding my wrists and ankles. Two hours and they'd be back to bump me off. What were these weirdos plotting? Who—or what—the hell was Martin? Why'd they steal and kill all these rare guitars? It pissed me off plenty.

There was a hullabaloo in the big room beyond the locked door. Someone was making a speech. A crowd was clapping, then came music—electronic stuff. The melody was familiar in a strange way. What was that song?

A crack of light shone beneath the door. A woman's voice piped up. It seemed right outside. The voice was one I'd heard before, but I couldn't place it right away. The crack of light blinked. Something slid underneath the door. It touched my ear. I thought it was a mouse. Three light bulbs flashed suddenly in my brain.

The song—it was a synthesizer version of "Deutschland Über Alles," sounding like two dozen robots on methedrine. The voice—it was Shirley's, the vinyl-clad vamp who'd lured me into this mess. The thing on the floor next to my ear—it was a knife.

Now if I could only reach over and...

The door swung open.

Chapter 4

Night Train to Nowhere

TWO NAKED WOMEN STOOD in galvanized tubs of water playing the theme from *Star Wars* on saxophones while a third woman dipped her bare feet in pots of paint and danced across a large canvas. A video crew recorded the performance on a State Arts Council grant and fifty suckers who'd doled out ten bucks apiece for entry were watching. Then the ceiling opened up and a guy clutching a knife dropped down, kicking over the paint pots and knocking one of the naked broads out cold. The audience clapped politely.

Standing on the West Broadway sidewalk, dripping paint, I flagged a cab and headed uptown to spend the night in a hideaway flophouse where nobody asks you any questions. Pointy, Sphinx, and their gang would be wise to my usual downtown haunts. And any minute they'd find the ripped up floorboards and the guy who had walked into that little room looking for the john all tied up and gagged. Soon those crazy nuts would hit the bricks crying for blood.

Two matters had to be settled right away. One was to find Shirley, my only alibi in the Ike Schmidt murder. The other was to telephone my client with the bad news about his missing axe so I could dump this lousy case. Everything about it was getting on my nerves: that weird loft, the Nazi music, all those sabotaged guitars. Too many numbers and they just didn't add up. I wanted my last paycheck. I wanted out.

For a week I lay low, dialing London every chance I got. The answer was the same each time: client out of town, touring with the band. First he was in France, then Italy, then Australia and New Zealand. Finally, over breakfast in a Lexington Avenue Blarney Stone, I cracked open the *Daily News* to discover my client had been busted for reefer and locked in a Tokyo slammer. If you want to know the truth, working for rock stars is nothing but headaches.

Getting itchy, I decided to try to pin down Shirley. I began checking the clubs, keeping an eye out for Sphinx's mugs and the other eye on the target, for that night I got a tip she was spinning discs at intermission for the Wazmo Nariz gig at Irving Plaza, but all I caught was a bunch of dolts taken in by a third-rate Joe Cocker. Another night I checked out a report she was backstage at the Palladium on Fourteenth Street, recharging batteries for Gary Numan's robots. All I found was Nash the Slash and other assorted mod automatons.

Shirley was a no-show all over town.

I walked into Tier 3 on a wet Thursday night. A trio called the Cyborgs was beeping and booping through a carefully programmed synthesizer set. A handful of people were dancing halfheartedly.

"Terrible, aren't they." said Simeon, a small blond guy who booked the bands. It was less of a question than a statement.

"Why'd you book them?"

"Find me something better."

I named half a dozen bands. He shook his head sadly.

'They're guitar bands. A dying breed. You can't find them anymore. There's not a guitar band playing anywhere in the city."

Sure enough, everywhere I went—Trax, Heat, CBGB, the '80s, Hurrah, Irving Plaza—the electronic boys had taken over. The whole music scene in New York was completely dominated by synthesizers.

"*Ay caramba!*" complained Joe "King" Carrasco over beer and nachos at a Mexican joint too good to name. Joe's not the complaining type, but he and his band, The Crowns, were in town from Austin, Texas, and having trouble.

"They stole my guitar. Now we can't play."

"Who stole it?" I asked.

"I don't know. It was a Fender Telecaster. It makes me very mad."

"Go up to Forty-Eighth Street and buy a new one."

"Didn't you hear, man? All the guitar shops on Forty-Eighth Street were firebombed last week!"

"What about the Third Avenue pawnshops?"

"Somebody pulled all the guitars shops out of hock. Every electric guitar in the whole city has disappeared. *Muy malo*. I've got to go back to Texas."

A few phone calls confirmed it. Like it was hit by some kind of disease, the city's guitar population had been wiped out. I was just flashing on all those guitars stashed in that weird loft with Sphinx and Pointy when, opening up the *Post*, I saw that Tokyo had cut my client loose and sent him back to London. I chucked a dime in the phone and dialed the overseas operator. She made the connection.

"'Ello?"

It was a smooth, Liverpudlian accent, a voice known to more people than the Pope's. I outlined the situation. He said he didn't care what condition the guitar was in, he wanted it back and he'd pay me an extra two grand to get it, plus expenses. Rock stars think they can buy anything. Sometimes they're right.

Three nights in a row I spent slouched in a doorway like a Bowery bum. In my fist was a bottle of Night Train. Across the street was the loft where Sphinx did whatever he was doing. I was searching for a way in. The fourth night I found it. Dozens of people were trooping up to the door, ringing the buzzer. They gave some kind of code word before the door opened up. Looked like another one of those meetings. Pulling my hat down over my face, I decided to attend.

It wasn't difficult to blend in with the crowd going up the old freight elevator. An excited buzz was in the air, like something special was on tonight's agenda. We reached the floor and went in. Pointy was standing guard, but he didn't notice me.

The room was packed with a funny sort of crowd. Half of them were Krauts or Brits, all dressed mod with crew cuts in tight, dark suits and Dave Clark boots. I recognized members of The Cyborgs and Nash the Slash. I took a seat with the others. There must have been nearly a hundred people, all sitting, waiting. For what? I measured the distance between the little room where the guitars were stashed and where I was sitting.

All of a sudden there was that music again: a synthesizer rendition of "Deutschland Über Alles." Everyone stood up and Nazi saluted. I did likewise. From behind a red curtain, out stepped Sphinx, all dolled up in a black uniform. A shoulder patch displayed two F-sharp notes in the form of jagged lightning bolts. The music quit. He motioned everyone to sit down.

"Our campaign so far," he announced, "has been as successful as we planned. At the present time, not one electric guitar exists within the city. Electronic music reigns supreme!"

The crowd applauded furiously.

"But we will not stop here," he continued. "There are greater heights to scale. And so now, as I promised, you will see for the first time our secret weapon. With this weapon we will invade the hearts and minds of the public, conquer the music industry, and guarantee Top-40 hits for electronic music for decades to come!"

More fanatical clapping.

"The man you are about to meet is a genius, the son of a world-famous man who knew what true leadership was about. For years, he has labored in the remote jungles of South America, aided by the best minds of a brilliant, but fugitive regime. Now, at last, he comes to us bringing a fabulous secret weapon."

Sphinx tugged and the curtains feel aside.

"Friends," he declared, "please welcome Martin Bormann, Jr.!!"

There he stood a chubby, little creep peering through a pair of specs with lenses thicker than coke bottles. Even so, his eyes projected a mad gleam. He turned to a keyboard, punched out a few high notes that squeezed through a dozen circuits, twisted around fifty condensers, bounced off a hundred microchips, and entered the human ear like red-hot scalpels. It was an eerie performance.

The little maniac soaked up the applause, then held his hands in the air for quiet. "For many centuries," he began, "musicians all over the world have sought the perfect tune. The Greeks called it the

Orpheus Scale—a three-chord sequence so perfect, so matched to the rhythms of the human body, pitched so exactly to the brain's own electronic impulses that it would instantly hypnotize all who listened.

"Ten years ago, in the jungles of Peru, I came upon a Mayan temple. Inside that temple were many wonderful paintings and hieroglyphs describing the musical entertainments of that magnificent lost culture. Among those inscriptions was the score of a Mayan holy song, the title of which, when I translated it, was "Don't Play Me." *Why?* I wondered. Until finally, aided by computers, I deciphered the song itself. It contained three almost impossible chords in sequence—the Orpheus Scale! With it, any musician can rule the world. Together, we shall do exactly that!"

He pointed a fat finger at a table stacked with papers.

"There," he said, "is the blueprint for world conquest. Sheet music containing the three-chord sequence embedded in my own updated version of "Don't Play Me." Before you leave here, each of you will take that sheet music, practice it with your bands, go out to the new wave clubs, and play it. But don't forget: whenever you play "Don't Play Me" wear earplugs, or the three-chord sequence will paralyze you as it paralyzes your audience."

There was a break for refreshments. Lots of Heineken beer and schnitzel. The guy next to me was lighting a cigarette. It gave me an idea. It was a desperate tactic, but it had to work or the whole world would literally be up to its ears in trouble.

The guy let me bum a smoke. I palmed his butane lighter. Reaching into my pockets I dug out a rubber band, a paper clip, and a pack of matches. Working quickly and using my hat for cover, I fashioned a serviceable version of what the bomb squad calls a Puerto Rican hand grenade. The lit cigarette wedged into the matchbook made a perfect time-delay fuse. While everybody was milling around, I edged over to the table with the sheet music, then I backed away. I bumped into something. It was Pointy, or rather it was Pointy's gun.

"Looking for something?" he grinned. I wanted to bust him in the harelip, but Sphinx appeared similarly armed.

"I hope you enjoyed our little presentation tonight," said Sphinx. "Because it's the last thing you'll ever enjoy. Take him away, Pointy."

They would have taken me away, too, if the whole back of the loft hadn't exploded into a mass of flames. I gave Pointy a karate kick to the heart that would have felled Bruce Lee. Sphinx ran to save the sheet music, but it was too late. I went after him but he disappeared in the mad crush of people struggling to escape the fire that was rapidly engulfing the loft. Next thing I knew, a heavy part of the ceiling collapsed and I was surrounded by smoke, blaze, and waves of burning heat, so I dove blindly into a solid sheet of flame in a crazed effort to find a way out of certain death...

Chapter 5

Manic Panic

FIVE TOURISTS FROM LONG Island with their newly purchased seven-by-nine photo-realist painting of a red stop sign from the R. J. Plimpton Gallery were struggling down West Broadway. Now my theory is that at birth each of us gets an allotment of luck. Some guys use it up over a lifetime of dice, cards, slow horses, and fast women. Me—I used up my share in thirty seconds crashing through the fifth story window of a burning loft building on West Broadway, landing in the middle of five open-mouthed tourists using a seven-by-nine-foot photo-realist painting as a trampoline.

Fire trucks were roaring up, sprouting ladders, hoses, and shouting firemen. I was on my feet in time to catch a quick glimpse of Sphinx and Pointy. They hustled chubby little Martin Bormann, Jr. into a yellow step van and tore off down the street. The rest of their gang got away as best they could. I could have cared less about the keyboard Kaisers; as long as Bormann's deadly sheet music was up in smoke, I figured the world was still safe for rock and roll.

Unfortunately, all those rare guitars stashed in the loft were also in ashes. But what the hell—it solved the case for me. All I had to do was call my client, tell him the guitar he'd hired me to track down was now destroyed, collect my fee, and get good and drunk.

Last things first. I was settled in at Club 57 with a couple of shots of bourbon under my belt. Scully was spinning some fine discs and the place was jumping. On the wall, an old Indy 500 film was reeling. Mario Andretti was explaining the finer points of an overhead camshaft. The bourbon was just about reaching my toenails. Everything was hunky-dory—until two plainclothesmen strolled in. You could tell they were cops; they were the only guys in the club with long hair.

They bellied up to the bar and began bending ears. I figured they were asking about me when Ann the bartender shot me a look that said "scram." I slipped out the door when the fuzz wasn't looking.

A dance party at the St. Marks Bar & Grill was full swing. I was relaxing with a beer in the corner, chatting up a purple-haired sweetie from Jersey who swore she knew Eno personally. The jukebox was pouring out "Cold Sweat" by James Brown. Everything was fine—until two plainclothes dicks ambled into the room. You could tell they were cops; they were the only ones in the crowd wearing real ties. I pulled my hat down over my eyes and ducked out the backdoor.

Over at the UK Club on the Bowery, Pierce Turner and Larry Kirwan were laboring to explain why they'd changed the name of their group from "Turner and Kirwan of Wexford" to "Major Thinkers." All I wanted to know was why I was being charged two bucks for a Bud. Copperfield, the owner, said, "Sorry, Ford. But this is an after-hours joint. Look who's walked in."

"You can tell they're cops," whispered Pierce. "They're the only ones with tweed overcoats that fit."

I took the backdoor route again. The boys in blue would give me no rest until the murderer of Ike Schmidt was collared. I had to get hold of Shirley and turn her in.

I dropped in at the Manic Panic. "She's not here," said Tish.

"I haven't seen her," said Snooky.

I poked my head backstage at Trax. "Not here," said Lydia Lunch. George, tuning up his bass, shook his head likewise.

"Nada," said the Romanian ticket taker at Squat. Inside, through the smoke and noise, I found Defunkt's Joseph Bowie wiping the spit off his horn. No, he hadn't seen her either.

"What do you wanna know for?" asked James Chance, his string-bean form folded malignantly into a too-big chair backstage at Hurrah. But he was just bluffing. As I was leaving, Jack the bouncer pulled me aside.

"There's someone been axing 'bout you, man."

He nodded toward the stairwell. She was standing in the shadows, a vision in skintight-pink spandex and stiletto heels.

"Hello, Ford," Shirley purred.

She looked good, too good. I wanted to grab her and say a lot of things about the moon in June, but it was the middle of March and we were both out in the cold.

"C'mon," I growled, taking her by the arm. "You played me for a sap once," I told her. "This time I'm taking you downtown. You've got a date with the DA."

"You don't understand," she said, big tears rolled down her cheeks leaving wide tracks of mascara. I felt sorry for her.

"Stop your sobbing."

"That's just a song by The Pretenders," she wept.

And a remake at that, I thought, searching for something nice to say. I remembered the tough spot she'd gotten me out of.

"Thanks for slipping me the knife at Sphinx's loft."

"See? I helped you," she said. "Can't you help me now? If you turn me in I'll never get my brother back. Don't you understand? The whole reason I've been hanging around the clubs in New York is to find my poor little brother. He disappeared from Cleveland six months ago. I looked all over for him. Then I heard he was playing in Sphinx's band, so I came here. He's too young to be running around the clubs. He hardly knows what's he's doing. If I could just see him, talk to him for only a minute—but he's like a prisoner. Sphinx's gang won't let me near poor Fred."

"Poor Fred, huh?" I asked, and told her, "Look, sister, we're traveling downtown."

"Oh, Ford, please you've got to believe me. If you help me rescue Fred, I promise I'll turn myself in to the police."

"Why shouldn't I turn you in right now?"

"Because—because I didn't kill Ike Schmidt and only my bother Fred knows who the real murderer is."

Something in her eyes said she wasn't fibbing. If her brother really was a material witness, then that might prove one more ace up my sleeve when the DA got around to grilling me on the Schmidt case. I decided to give her one more chance, but this time I'd stick to her like gaffer's tape.

We ate dinner at Lucky Linda's Caribe Café on West Ninety-Fourth in the middle of Little Haiti. Photos of Baby Doc Duvalier stuck full of darts adorned the walls and every seat in the place had a clear shot at the front door.

"This is kind of romantic," whispered Shirley.

"Son of Sam used to eat here all the time," I schooled her. "Mick Jagger, too."

"Wow. Like, it's so dangerous."

"It's a dangerous decade, baby."

And there are all sorts of ways a guy like me takes risks.

***

IT WAS LATE WHEN we left my hotel. We moseyed down Broadway. Bums begged for quarters. Reggae blared from a storefront. The night settled in on the Upper West Side like a welfare family, all spread out, sullen, and threatening to be permanent.

A bent character carrying a paste pot, brush, and knapsack full of paper paused on the corner of Eighty-Eighth. It was Flakey Jake, the guy who puts up posters all over town for rock bands. They say he eats too much wheat paste and it's made him wacko.

"Who's playing tonight, Jake?" I asked, reaching for one of the posters in his sack. Jake jumped back a foot and looked menacing.

"You can't read the poster until I put it up!" he hissed.

We watched him slop the poster on the wall with his wet brush, lick the excess paste off, and slink away, muttering darkly.

"Look!" cried Shirley. "The Fourth Reich is playing the Mudd Club tonight at midnight!"

"Never heard of them."

"That's Sphinx's band! We've got to go there and rescue Fred!"

And stop Martin Bormann, Jr. who, no doubt, intended to unleash the Orpheus Scale on the club's unsuspecting audience this very night. It would be Sphinx's first step toward world domination. And we had only thirty minutes to get downtown to stop him.

"What are you doing?" screamed Shirley as I kicked in the window of the nearest parked car.

"Get inside and shut up," I ordered.

Underneath the dashboard, I hot-wired the ignition. The car fired right up. We shot across intersections like Magic Johnson going for a layup. Cabbies swerved out of the way. Bus drivers stomped their brakes. Every pimpmobile in Times Square stopped dead to let us by. Two cop cars at Forty-Second Street blocked the way.

"Hold on."

We rammed them head-on, knocking them out of the way. By the time we reached Herald Square, the city was alive with sirens. I turned left and headed east on Thirty-Fourth, turned right on Park, doubled back on Thirtieth, passed two cops going the other way, and turned south again on Seventh Avenue. I guessed they'd be putting up roadblocks at Sheridan Square, but it was a chance we had to take. With six cop cars in back of us and who knows what lay ahead, we had only fifteen minutes to get downtown and prevent the worst disaster since Altamont.

Chapter 6

A Sunnyview of Life

STOP—*OOYAH*! STOP—*OOYAH*!"

Bullhorn burped warnings. Barricades blocked off the avenue ahead. Cops swarmed across the dirty sidewalk like gnats on an open wound. I checked the speedometer; it was nudging ninety. I checked Shirley. She was nineteen going on thirty-eight. If this didn't work I could be doing eight-to-ten—or else we'd both be six feet under. A hundred-to-one chance we could get away with it. I looked at the speedometer again. The numbers computed in that slot machine I call a brain. It came up cherries. As Van Morrison says, it's too late to stop now, so I pushed the girl underneath the dashboard and Evel Knieveled the accelerator.

Wood shattered. Glass broke. Things flew in the air. The steering wheel lurched with a mind of its own as we hurtled over sidewalks and people, and shotgun blasts ripped into steel. Blind, raging instincts jerked my arm to the right. The vehicle obeyed with a sullen thud, the sound of pavement punching rubber. Blue uniforms scattered. In a moment we were on the riverfront, roaring downtown without a cop in sight.

Shirley eyed her makeup in the rearview mirror. "Can't you go any faster?" she asked. "We've only got five minutes."

On Walker Street we abandoned the car. It would take the police a few minutes to catch up. We crossed the cobbled street past the Baby Doll Lounge with its blinking lights, past the warehouses and loft buildings with their shadowy fronts and co-op signs. Suddenly a shadow moved. It moved from a doorway to the sidewalk and stood there grinning with a knife. It was Sphinx's henchman, Pointy.

"Watch out, Ford!" Shirley screamed.

He came at me with a swipe that went wild. I caught his knife hand but he jerked loose and knocked me to the asphalt. When he lunged for my throat, I grabbed his foot and he went down. I was up in a fraction of a second, came down on his chest with all my weight and both knees. The wind poured out, foul and fetid. He gnashed his decaying teeth. His harelip curled back and he spit

"Thon of a bitch!"

The knife came up again. Shirley yelled. The blade sliced through cloth and flesh between my knee and ankle. Wetness soaked my shoe. Shirley handed me a length of lead pipe and I caved the monster's head in.

Not a minute to soon, we reached the Mudd Club. A band was audibly tuning up inside. A big crowd was waiting to be allowed in. The guy at the door was, as usual, being picky. We pushed to the front.

"Where do you think you're going?"

"Inside."

"That's what you think."

"But we know Steve Mass."

"That's what they all say." He grinned at the mention of the owner's name with all the dumb smugness that growing up rich and bored in the suburbs can give a guy. I gave him my special knuckle sandwich. It was like shoving my hand in a bowl of oatmeal. He crumpled to the sidewalk with a soft thud. We went inside.

"For our first number," said a voice over the PA, "here's a little song called 'Don't Play Me.'"

Martin Bormann, Jr. stood poised at the synthesizer. The band was ready to play that song—the song that would unleash a terrible force on the world and perhaps even end it. Sphinx, the mastermind, was at the foot of the stage. He saw us coming and commanded The Fourth Reich to play. Martin Bormann, Jr., with a wicked gleam in his eye, plunged a fat finger onto the keyboard and at the same time Shirley screamed. "Fred!"

She rushed to the stage, knocking over amps, tossing mikes across the floor while the musicians tried to stop her. I saw horror write itself in big letters on Sphinx's face. He saw her lurching toward the keyboards. With her bare hands, the frantic girl ripped cords right out of the sockets, yanked out jacks and wires until they tangled around her body like snakes, hissing with live voltage.

"Don't...!" Sphinx started to shout. But it was too late. Two of the writhing snakes kissed. There was a flash of light, a rain of hot sparks, and the room was thrown into screaming mayhem. The lights blinked out. Fists clawed the air. Bottles crashed against the walls. The room reverberated with the sound of heads cracking. I saw Sphinx duck out the back way, and I went after him.

Up the alley he ran, the dim light throwing his crooked shadow against the dirty walls. A truck was parked at the end of the alley. Sphinx whipped open the door, jumped behind the wheel, and revved the engine. I was trapped. The truck came at me. There was nowhere to go but up—up on the hood. I landed on my stomach on the hood as the truck wheeled down the narrow passage. Sphinx jogged the wheel, trying to shake me loose, but I grasped the windshield wipers. Pulling myself up to the window, I reached into the cab and spun the wheel around. The truck slid against the brick, then emerged onto the street where it plowed into two cop cars and came to a halt. The boys in blue, pistols drawn, surrounded us.

"What's going on here?" bellowed the police captain, a thickset red-haired character named Regan. I showed him my PI license.

"You fool!" hissed Sphinx, in the grip of two burly cops. "I could have ruled the world with my music."

"You're finished."

"Sphinx?" said the captain, scrutinizing the noseless man. "Hell, that's Ernie the Gypper. He's got a record as long as the BMT. Fraud, counterfeiting, assault and battery, mail theft—you name it."

"Hey, Captain. Look at this!"

The cop was pointing inside the truck. We took a look. Stacked up on neat rows like so much cordwood were three or four thousand electric guitars—the entire city's worth of swiped axes. I could make out a 1958 Stratocaster with burgundy metallic finish, a 1959 ES Dotmarker Gibson (probably worth over two grand), a 1964 Trini Lopez Custom model with a cherry sunburst finish and a firebird headstock. There was a pink-paisley Telecaster, a 1949 Emperor Varitone with three pick-ups, and a 1964 Sheraton, the kind they don't make anymore with two Epiphone humbuckers. There were plenty of sharp custom jobs: a blue, silver-sparkle Kawai Moon; a Jeff Levin Sardonyx; a 1968 Intergalactic with four pick-ups and a laser attachment, and a Zemaitis with an engraved metal front that looked exactly like the one Keith Richards played. And there, sitting on top of the whole pile, was the Link Wray lyre–body Danelectro that had gotten me into all this trouble in the first place.

"Well, Ford. You've got what you wanted. So did I."

It was Shirley. And Martin Bormann, Jr. She pointed to him and said, "Meet my brother, Fred."

"What th—?"

"Fred escaped six months ago from Sunny-view Farm."

"That's a looney bin," said Fred matter-of-factly.

"Right," said Shirley. "He was once a child prodigy at the piano. But then Fred took LSD and had a bum trip. He became convinced that he was the son of Martin Bormann. He also got hung up on playing the same three chords. So when he came to New York, he joined a group, fell in with Sphinx, and..."

That explained everything. Almost. "What about Ike Schmidt?"

Fred brightened up. "Sphinx did it," he said. "I saw him put a funny powder in a little piece of paper that he put in Ike's pocket."

"He's not so crazy," I said. Fred repeated the story to Captain Regan.

"Guess that lets you off the hook, Fairlane," said the cop. He clapped the irons on Sphinx. "Let's go," he said. "There's a special place for punks like you up in Attica."

"Have you heard my new single?" Fred said, handing me a record. It was by The Fourth Reich and titled "Don't Play Me." I let him autograph the sleeve before Shirley led him away.

He went back to the laughing academy. She went back to Cleveland. I stayed out every night at the clubs, drinking her memory away. I gave Fred's single to Jim Fouratt who runs Danceteria. I told him about the Orpheus Scale. We both had a good laugh.

Then, just for a joke, Jim played it one night at the club. Of course, the crowd was crazy about it. That's how it broke into the charts. All the rock critics wrote about the song's distinctive hook, a peculiar sequence of three chords. "Almost hypnotic in its effect," wrote Lester Bangs.

"Electrifying," said John Morthland.

Now I can't go anywhere without hearing those same, damned three chords. Over and over and over again.

LOS ANGELES

Chapter 1

The Snatch

THE SKY OVER CHINATOWN was thick and heavy. The air smelled like Tommy Lasorda's sweat socks. The sweet and pungent pork pawed at my intestines. We made too much noise walking across the empty parking lot. My hatband was too tight. I'd been in LA too long. Ronald Reagan was running for president. Blame it on the bossa nova. Blame what happened that night on a million wrong things.

Not, however, that I wasn't doing my job.

As we walked toward the car, my hand rested on the Ruger in my shoulder holster. I kept the girl in my shadow. A couple of hours ago she was skidding across tables at Madame Wong's eat-to-the-beatery, knocking over people's drinks with her mike stand, and hiccuping a fair version of rockabilly. Now, in her leopard-skin leotard and red spiked heels she stepped silently beside me. If the lead singer of Wanda and the Whips was afraid, she wasn't saying. My job was to get her home from the gig without a scratch and tuck the little blonde punk into bed.

I'd told the voice on the phone I didn't bodyguard. I hadn't given up a good job as head bouncer at Hurrah's in New York City to go through all you have to go through to get a private detective's license (#096422) just to be somebody's babysitter. Besides, my time in LA was all booked up with pool lounging, beer drinking, and other heavy stuff. Call me tourist, okay?

The voice on the phone wouldn't compute that input. "I'm her manager," he huffed, "and I've invested a lot in Wanda. I'm sending her to London on her first European tour and I don't want anybody to mess her up, especially that loser boyfriend of hers. He sweeps the studio for the Eagles. She's going to be a star."

"So's the maid at the Magic Motel," said I, winking at old Clara who was dragging the laundry off the floor of my room.

"But, you've got a responsibility," he said. "You're the only private eye in the rock business." He then sketched a very big dollar sign for the nursemaid job. I asked him to double it. He did. I suddenly decided to become responsible.

The drive across LA was a piece of cake. By the time we hit Sunset, she had the FM dialed to Rodney's show on KROQ. She was snapping her fingers to D-Day's rendition of "Too Young to Date." When I parked the car in the garage of the Chateau Marmont she wouldn't let me switch off the ignition until the song was over.

On the way up to her room, I eyeballed every nook and crevice for hidden thugs. No such luck. The night clerk at the front desk gave us the once over. He was reading *The Shining*. Around the corner was room fifteen. Wanda's manger chose it, he said because it was safely within sight of the front desk.

I turned the key in the lock, thinking of the six-pack waiting for me back at the Magic Motel. The door sprang open and my job was just about over. It was a pretty big suite for such a little girl. Wanda went to open a window. Before going home to that six-pack, I decided to sniff out the rooms. Kitchen, fully equipped. Bathroom, stocked with thick towels on the rack. Two walk-in closets. Living room with TV console. Two more closets. Another bathroom. And a big bedroom with somebody I didn't see behind the door who cracked me on the skull with a piece of hardwood that rolled down all my curtains.

Was it that jack-in-the-box I use for a brain, or did I really hear Wanda laughing? Or was she screaming?

Chapter 2

The Funny Joke

H OT AGAINST MY CHEEK, the bedroom carpet rippled wall-to-wall, stirred by sunlight poking through the curtains. My eyes adjusted. I tried to sit up. There was a bass drum beating four-four time between my ears. It was going to be hours before Godzilla took his paw off the foot pedal. I decided to get a few questions answered in the meantime.

No, the desk clerk hadn't seen anything all night. Yes, my Rent-a-Wreck was still parked downstairs. No, Wanda's manager wasn't in, said the secretary: he was "taking a meeting." Yes, Schwab's drugstore down the street had a big bottle of aspirin for sale.

The bump on my head was still there after breakfast. That was bad. Worse was the fact that I'd bungled an easy job. Maybe Los Angeles was turning my brain into mush. Maybe it was the air, or lack of air, or something. But that was no excuse. There was only one thing to do—get Wanda back.

My first theory was simple. I called it the "boyfriend hypothesis." Wanda's manger had warned me about him. I figured the boyfriend didn't want to see Wanda go off on tour to London so he booked her on his own private tour. Find the boyfriend, I figured, and I'd find Wanda. I headed over to the manager's office to tell him my brilliant theory.

The address was on La Cienega. It was one of those two-story, beige-on-beige buildings designed sort of like cottage cheese on cantaloupe so as not to excite the ulcers of the high-strung bastards nine-to-fiving inside. I tucked the car in the back lot. A stairway led upstairs. On the way in, I was nearly bowled over by a couple of guys in a big hurry. I wouldn't have marked them but for two standouts. Both had heads shaved as close as tennis balls. One stomped my foot with a steel-tipped construction boot. A purring Trans Am swallowed them up and took off without so much as a 'scuse me.

The door said Mitch Mitchell Talent Inc. It was open. The reception area was standard management décor, a chorus of album covers and a duet of gold records. The receptionist's desk was empty. It was lunchtime. She was probably out spooning a low-cal snack. The silence seemed to be settling like thick dust. It made my nose itch. I took a peek around.

Mitch Mitchell's office was flooded with light. A large, airy place, it featured a plush sofa and leather chairs that said business was real good. In the middle was a slab of polished mirror that could have been the Jolly Green Giant's coke mirror. That was Mitch Mitchell's desk. Behind it was a high-backed swivel chair with built-in headphones straight out of *Star Wars*. That was Mitch Mitchell's chair. Underneath the desk was a pair of Gucci loafers with gold buckles. Those were Mitch Mitchell's shoes. Attached to the shoes was Mitch Mitchell. He didn't seem to be in any mood to hear the boyfriend hypothesis or any other theory. The front of his Armani suit was messed up by three fresh bullet holes. Mitch Mitchell was dead.

Somewhere, a bored cop on desk duty got an adrenalin surge from an anonymous tip about a stiff on La Cienega. That was me calling from a pay phone on La Brea, after wiping all my prints from Mitchell's office. Only those two skinheads had seen me going in there. But I'd seen them going out. I wondered about the skinheads. I wondered about Mitch Mitchell. I had to find out more. I called the only man who would know—radio personality, lead singer of Puke, and punk-about-town, Vin Vomsky.

"Meet me at the Starwood," Vin said. "Ten thirty. I'll be up front."

Lunch at Duke's. Pinball at Barney's Beanery. A steak dinner at Port's. Booze and nine-ball at the Raincheck. By then it was 10:30 p.m. When you've got time to kill, LA is a willing accomplice.

Ron the ticket taker waved me in the door at the Starwood. I elbowed through the packed crowd. Vomsky was right where he said he'd be, standing at the front. His stocky figure was braced against the crush, fist clenched around a bottle of Bud.

"You're gonna catch a good show tonight," he said. "Darby Crash. He's great."

I asked him about Mitchell.

"Mitch Mitchell? His specialty is taking punk bands that are good and rough, smoothing the edges, rounding off the riffs, and turning them into mainstream pop bands that suck. He's responsible for every Knack and Cars clone in the city. He discovered the formula for turning gold into shit and he's making a fucking fortune."

"Does he have any enemies?"

"Does the Pope pogo? Mitch Mitchell is the Shah of new wave." *In more ways than one*, I thought.

"Who hates him most?"

"South Bay beach punks are pissed off at Mitchell 'cause he ruined half their best bands. Long-haired rockers of The Eagles variety hate him 'cause he's muscling them out of the picture. And just about every coke dealer in town."

"Why's that?"

"Hoover nose don't pay his bills."

The crowd erupted in angry little knots. Darby Crash strode across the stage and picked his mike off the stand. His Mohawk bristled like a porcupine's quills. Dead animal skins and feathers dangled from his leather shirt and pants. Indian war paint streaked the shaved parts of his skull and pasty face. The band kicked off and Darby's vocals boxed my ears. The crowd splintered in crab-dancing, arm-flailing pogoers.

Bodies ricocheted across the room. Vomsky and I retreated to the upstairs balcony.

In the middle of Darby's set, two plainclothes cops walked in the door. You could tell they were cops because they were the only ones wearing wide ties. They scanned the joint, knowing what they were looking for. The next thing I knew, Lieutenant Keeler of the LAPD Homicide Squad was introducing himself and Lieutenant Chow at our table. He had to yell in my ear over Darby's music.

"I'll tell you a funny joke," said Keeler. "A guy was found dead in his office. He had three bullets in him. But he told us who the killer was anyway. Guess how?"

I said I didn't give a shit.

"You will. You see, the dead guy wrote a name and phone number on his note pad just as he was dying. The name was Ford Fairlane. Isn't that funny?"

"This guy's got a warped sense of humor," said Vin.

"Shut up," growled Chow.

"Anyway," smiled Keeler, "the punch line is we're taking you in on suspicion of murder. Let's go, Ford"

Going downstairs, I was wedged between the two cops. Vin disappeared. Just as we hit the dance floor, Darby Crash unleashed a brilliant rendition of "Beyond Help." The crowd contracted massive epilepsy. Suddenly, the two cops and I were stuck in the mosh pit in the midst of pushing, shoving, writhing bodies. The cops were scared. They grabbed my arms and tried to move in the direction of the door.

A body came hurtling through space. It smacked into Keeler, bounced off and slammed into Chow, sending them both to the floor. It was Vomsky. About twenty pogo maniacs piled on top, still wriggling to the music. From the bottom of the pile, Vin poked his head out and yelled above the noise.

"Run, man, run!"

Chapter 3

The Connection

THE COPS WOULD INFEST the neighborhood any minute. I had my motor humming.

But the corner of Sweetzer and Santa Monica was choked with cars. It was Saturday night and everybody in LA had a place to go. Even if it was no place.

I wheeled my heap across the sidewalk. A garbage can went flying off the curb. Drivers jammed on their brakes. Traffic parted like the Red Sea. I charged across the street, burning rubber, bending fenders, and doing Earl Scheib a couple of favors. Horns blew, but nobody tried to stop me as I sped away, heading south.

One street looked just like the other. In five minutes, I was in a maze of two-story plaster villas that made one block the carbon copy of the other. I was lost. I had to find Wanda's boyfriend somehow, but my only plan at the moment was to put distance between me and the sirens gathering around the Starwood. Then somebody had a different idea.

"Turn left at the corner and then drive straight ahead. Don't look back or you're dead," said a voice from the back seat. Cold iron pressed against back of my skull. I never argue with cold iron.

"Stop here."

We halted in a shadowed spot underneath a wild jasmine bush. The smell was life or death.

"Where is she?"

"Who?"

The cold iron pressed harder. "Don't play games. I know you've got Wanda. Man, I oughta just blow your damn head off right here."

Taking a chance, I checked the rearview mirror. A face framed with long blond hair that stared back at me. He was holding a gun. The boyfriend. The one who did session work for The Eagles.

"I thought you had Wanda," I said.

"You think I'm not playing with all my strings, don't you?" he said, his voice soggy with 'ludes. "You think I don't know what's going down. That fat loudmouth Mitchell. Well, I'm going to shut him up for good."

"Somebody beat you to it, pal."

The gun quivered. "What do you mean, man?"

Boyfriend was for real. I figured if I had to tell him that Mitchell was croaked, then he couldn't have had anything to do with it. Add the quaalude factor, and it summed up to four letters: wimp.

"Like, don't mess with my head," he was saying. "I just want you to tell me where Wanda is." His voice was sobby. "I just want my Wanda back. I love the bitch. I'm gonna marry her. But Mitchell hired you to keep me away from her, didn't he?"

"Yeah," I said, feeling the gun shaking in his hand as he tried to keep it pointed at my head. "But now Mitchell's dead and the cops think I did it. I was trying to find you because I thought you did it."

"Wait a minute, man. Like, I'm all confused."

That was good because I swung around, clamped my elbow over his gun, shoved my hand edgewise into his Adam's apple, and stunned the sucker flat out across the back seat. I picked his heater up off the floor and drew my own.

"Wow, man. Like, you didn't have to hit so hard."

A blue-black bruise was spreading across his neck.

"Time's not on our side," I said. "Now, if you don't have Wanda and I don't have Wanda, where is she?"

"We gotta find her, man. I love the bitch."

I suggested we start looking around in the places where Wanda usually hung out. Maybe somebody would know something. The boyfriend agreed.

"Sorry about the gun, man. But I'm ultra-mad at Wanda for disappearing like this. My name's Strat. Strat Kaster."

Strat Kaster hopped in the front seat and we took off. First stop: the Whisky. On the way, Strat popped a couple of dexies and turned from 'lude head into motormouth.

"...and so I'm not into new wave or punk so much. I'm more into Jackson Browne, The Eagles, Nicolette Larson, that kind of thing. I played backup on Linda Ronstadt's new album. But I promised Wanda I was going to get a punk haircut just for her."

We parked the car on the Strip. The usual sharks and piranhas were prowling the sidewalks hungry for action. Pat at the door of the Whisky waved me and Strat inside.

On stage, the twenty-two-year-old rockabilly genius Colin Winski was working up a sweat. He churned through "Burning Desire." The young girls grabbed for his legs. He sank to his knees and barked like a dog. With a baby face like that a guy could get away with anything.

A looker with Jayne Mansfield hair in a tight black dress with see-through top and high heels stood off to the side. It was my old friend Happy Daye. She's the Rona Barrett of the LA club scene.

"'Lo, Ford," she said. "New York get too cold for you?"

"Yeah, and now LA's too hot. Know Wanda of Wanda and the Whips?"

"She was here about a half hour ago."

"Where'd she go?"

"Try Madame Wong's West. She likes Billy Falcon's group and they're playing tonight. But, Ford..."

"What?'

"Be careful. The word's out. You're playing with fire."

"I don't burn easily," I said, and she smiled.

Strat kept jabbering as we walked out the door. "Wanda's my girl, man. I play better than them, man. I mean, I'm going to wise her up when I see her. She's in bad company, man. Bad company."

In front of Tower Records, a black Dodge Charger came down the hill cruising west. If I'd been paying more attention, I would have seen the long, black nose of an AK-47 poking through the rear window. As it was, I had just enough time to yell "Get down!" and roll into the gutter while the lead coughed against the sidewalk. My left arm turned numb. A searing pain crossed my chest. There were exactly twenty-seven stars in the LA sky that night.

Chapter 4

Like Falling Off A Cliff

"YOU OKAY?" I HEARD somebody ask.

The pain was sharp. Not bullet sharp, but something else. I lifted myself off the dirty asphalt. A fractured Heineken bottle lay in the gutter, jagged side up, covered with the same blood that stained my shirtfront. I'd survived a machine-gunning, but was nearly snuffed by a litterbug.

Strat grabbed my arm. "C'mon," he said, as sirens began to howl a few blocks away. "We've got to beat feet."

Happy Daye's tip that Wanda was at Madame Wong's West turned out to be late. I checked every inch of the place, a former prime-rib palace turned punk. The Twisters were playing. The crowd was doing a sort of Simon Says dance, wiggling arms and tilting their bodies in imitation of the band.

"Didn't Happy say that Billy Falcon was playing here tonight, and that Wanda was here to see him?" I asked Strat.

Strat pointed to a poster on the wall. "She gave us a bum tip. Falcon played here last week."

Why would Happy Daye lead me wrong on Wanda?

At the Club 88 on West Pico, we ran into more static. The Benders from Tulsa were doing their best to revive the Merseybeat. A couple of girls in vinyl miniskirts from Fred Segal were doing the jerk on the dance floor. Joel at the door was friendly until the name Wanda was mentioned. Then his face turned to slate.

At the other end of town, John Hiatt was finishing up his set at Madame Wong's Chinatown spot. The waitresses were jiving to "Pink Bedroom." The encore was "634-5789," delivered red-hot. Near the hand-carved teak bar—a remnant of a long-forgotten world's fair—a demure, middle-aged woman stood whispering to a young boy.

"That's Madame Wong," said Strat. "What she wants, she gets."

In a moment, the boy was at my side.

"Madame Wong wants to speak with famous detective, Ford Fairlane."

"Better go," said Strat. "I'll wait here."

In the dim light of her office, Madame Wong looked like anything but a dragon lady. Her soft face and tiny figure could have graced the cover of a travel brochure. But when she spoke, that singsong voice had an edge of iron.

"You are looking for something," said Madame Wong, pouring two cups of tea from a lacquered tray and offering me one. "And why have you come to my club?"

She smiled. Though I could tell she knew all the answers, I told her anyway. Her smile revealed nothing. She offered me a bowl of fortune cookies.

"I wish I could be of service," she said. "But unfortunately—please go on, help yourself."

I took a cookie from the bowl, not wanting to be rude.

"I too am fond of Wanda. One of my favorite bands," she said. "But you are looking in the wrong place."

"What is the right place?"

She shrugged. I opened my fortune cookie and glanced at the paper inside. It read: *Try Hollywood* and gave an address on North Cahuenga. I looked up at Madame Wong and her smile still gave nothing away. We talked music for a few minutes, then I thanked her and excused myself.

"One more thing," she said. "They say that bad company is worse than no company at all."

When I checked the main room, the band was packing up the amps and rolling the drum cases down the stairs one step at a time. Strat was gone. *Bad company?*

Hollywood twinkled in the dark like cheap jewelry on a fat dame's arm. The address on North Cahuenga turned out to be the Double Zone, an after-hours juke joint popular with the purple-haired set. The door opened to the right faces, and for a few bucks you could dance, get drunk, fall on the floor, and waste your brain cells until dawn.

When I walked in, the place was packed. The elite of LA's club scene was there: Kickboy Face and the *Slash* crowd, some ex-Germs, a few Screamers, a couple of Weirdos, and some visiting denizens of Skinhead Manor. Belinda of The Go-Go's, all dolled up in a pink party dress, sat at a corner table, touching up her lipstick. She caught my eye and waved me over.

"Well, if it isn't the detective from New York City," she said, snapping her compact shut. Her friends, seated around the table, giggled. "Have you found Wanda yet?"

I replied negative.

"You won't find her, you know."

"Why not?"

"Because you're from New Yawk. You don't understand Los Angeles," she said. "This is *our* town."

"Maybe you've got the beat," I said to the blonde lead singer, "but I've got a job to do."

The truth was that everything was coming up blanks. I drove around the city trying to figure it out. Who killed Mitch Mitchell? Who kidnapped Wanda? Who was trying to kill me? The letters on the Hollywood sign all turned into question marks. I decided to get some shut-eye. A phone call to Karl, the manager at the Magic Motel, confirmed my guess: the boys in blue were staking out the place. Karl was willing to sneak me in the back way and put me in a basement room, which is where I woke up twelve hours later with my nose being tickled by the business end of a machine gun.

"Get up slowly," said the owner of the weapon, "and put your hands behind your head."

"They made me do it, Ford!" Karl was trussed with rope on the floor.

"Shut up!" said one of the others. There were four of them standing in the room. Two of them I recognized. They looked like the ones I'd seen exiting Mitch Mitchell's office the day he was murdered. Like the ones who'd nearly filled my face with lead the other night on Sunset. Their heads were shaved close, like tennis balls. Their eyes were like cubes clicking at the dead end of a bar glass.

"Shut up!" said Skinhead Number One. "Wasting you guys would be easier to me than falling off a cliff."

Chapter 5

Mysteries of the Cuckoo's Nest

OVER IN THE CORNER, trussed like a Thanksgiving turkey, Karl groaned. By the look on his face, I guessed they'd left this part out of his hotel management course.

He wasn't the only one sweating. These guys meant business. Behind their eyes was an ugly movement, like, as the late Jim Morrison said, their brains were squirming toads.

"Okay," I said, tossing all my marked cards on the table, "you can wipe me out as a witness. But it's too late. The cops have your descriptions. They know I saw you coming out of Mitchell's office that day. They've got the place surrounded right now. I tipped them."

The skinheads stared. Would they swallow the bluff?

"What the Sam Hill is he talking about?" asked one.

"Got no idea," said the other.

"We don't know no Mitchell," said Skinhead Number Two. "We're just after your pal Strat Kaster.

He owes us plenty dough for a batch of 'ludes we sold him."

"We tried to blast him last night on Sunset, but you got in the way," laughed Skinhead Number Three. That put Wanda's boyfriend in a whole new light.

"I'll tell you where Strat is," I said, "but I'm telling you the cops are looking for two skinheads I saw leaving Mitch Mitchell's office three days ago."

"What'd they look like?"

I was going to tell them when the door suddenly began bouncing around on its hinges. "Police!" yelled a voice from the other side.

"If you guys want to get out of here, untie me, now!" said Karl. The skinheads loosened the ropes. Karl hauled out a giant ring of keys, selected one, and pulled back the throw rug. In the floor was a trapdoor. He unlocked it and we descended into a black hole.

"This tunnel was used by Janis Joplin to escape fans when she used to live in the hotel next door," said Karl. *That must be why*, I thought to myself, *this was called the Magic Motel*.

We emerged in the basement of the hotel next door. In a minute, we were tearing down La Brea in the skinheads' Dodge Charger. I had to talk fast now. I described the guys I'd seen coming out of Mitchell's office, every detail from the crew cuts to the chains on their construction boots.

"Which boot?" said Skinhead Number One.

"Which boot what?"

"The chain. Which boot was it on?"

"The left," I said.

Skinhead Number One cracked up. "This guy's a detective and he don't even know the difference between an LA skinhead and a South Bay punk!"

"See?" said the skinhead sitting next to me. He was pointing to his right boot. A thick steel chain snaked around the heel and ankle. "We wear 'em on the right. South Bay punks wear chains on the left."

"We hang out at the Starwood," said Skinhead Number Three. "Those guys hang out at the Cuckoo's Nest in Costa Mesa."

"That's exactly where the guy you're looking for is going to be tonight," I lied.

"Let's go," said the skinhead at the wheel, gunning the accelerator as he wheeled onto the Harbor Freeway on-ramp. They might not find Strat Kaster, but I'd get a chance to nail Mitchell's killers.

The cassette player was wound all the way up. Germs, Bags, Circle Jerks, Dead Kennedys, Urinals, poured out like molten steel. The skinheads passed around a paper bag full of Testor's and huffed themselves into toluene heaven. Near Torrance, we paused at Off-Ramp Liquors for a couple of six-packs.

Now we were really rolling down the big-wide 405. Once past the high-ticket hump of Palos Verdes, the wasteland began, a hellish strip of raped coastland carrying a rash of refineries, tract houses, used-car lots, trailer parks, and aerospace boondoggles on its sucked-out belly. It looked like the sort of place where you had a choice of lying back and dying a mellow death or getting up on your hind legs and screaming. Skinheads were in the last category, and it was getting dark.

We jumped off the freeway and headed toward the ocean. After Huntington Beach, the surfside shacks got funkier. The Pacific Coast Highway slid underneath the headlight beams. Finally, we turned left on Placentia and raced up to Seventeenth. A ribs and brew joint called Zubies, popular with hippie surfers, stood on the corner. Next door, set way back in a crowded parking lot, was a barn-like building swarming with kids...the Cuckoo's Nest.

A watery-eyed wimp name Marty worked the door. When asked for five bucks apiece, my companions just pushed him aside and we went in. The place was jammed. They were waiting for the band to come onstage, equipment all set up and everything.

"Who's playing?" I asked a kid.

"The Stinking Scumbunnies," said he. "They're the headliners. The band coming up now is Freda and the Frantics."

Suddenly, the crowd roared. The band walked onstage and grabbed their stuff. I recognized the bass player and the lead guitarist right away by their skinned heads and the chains on their left boots: the two guys who'd exited Mitchell's office. Then the lead singer came out and took the mike, a slim, blonde, spikey-haired girl I knew only too well. Freda and the Frantics was actually *Wanda* and the Murderers.

Their first song opened up like a sonic boom. No more rockabilly now, Wanda was taking Lydia Lunch out to dinner. Her voice rasped and wailed and drove the room into a frenzy. A guy over to my left began moving his arms like a propeller—a dance they call the slam. He slammed into somebody. Somebody else slammed back. In seconds, the floor was a battleground of brawling, bruising slammers slamming happily to the music.

But Marty the doorkeeper was pissed and chose that moment to bring in two long-haired bouncers who tried to put the arm on us for not paying. It was a mistake. Skinhead Number One pulled the machine gun out of his pants leg and loosed a few rounds into the ceiling. The lights flickered out. Punches flew. Next minute, the whole house was a bloody riot. Beach punks versus longhairs, who had rushed over from Zubies.

The band flew backstage. I followed. Wanda cowered in the dressing room. The two beach punks were packing up fast.

"Look," said one, "it's the detective."

"All three of you are coming with me," I said, drawing my .44. "I'm taking you two guys in for murdering Mitch Mitchell and kidnapping Wanda. You'll be in San Quentin for a couple of lifetimes."

"Drop it, Ford!" said a voice in back of me. I knew who it was before I turned around.

Chapter 6

The Permanent Chill

OUTSIDE THE DRESSING ROOM, the battle raged. Beer-bellied longhairs from Zubies Bar next door were piling in, lusting for a punch-up with the short-haired punks. The manager put on a Judy Collins record to try and calm everyone down, but it just made the punks meaner. It was mods versus rockers...sixties versus eighties.

In the room where we stood, the sound of fists crunching jawbones was muted.

The sound of a gun hammer being slowly pulled back and cocked drowned out everything else. The pistol felt icy against the back of my neck.

"Drop your piece, Ford," said the voice with a familiar quaalude drawl. I dropped it. The .44 hit the floor. A Frye boot kicked it out of reach. I was ordered to join the two punks against the wall at the same time that Wanda was told to walk forward slowly.

Strat Kaster grabbed the girl, pulling her to him, while keeping us covered. His eyes twitched. The gun shook in his hand. His mouth twisted into a smile.

"I knew if I followed you, you'd lead me right to her," he chuckled.

The two punks next to me looked nervous. The fight outside was growing louder.

Sirens wailed in the distance.

"Look," I said. "Why don't you and your girlfriend take off right now? The cops'll be here any minute. I'll make sure these two guys take the rap for Mitchell's murder."

"I'm afraid that's impossible," said Strat, twitching like a needle. "You don't seem to understand the situation."

"I'm *not* his girlfriend!" said Wanda.

"Shut up!" he snarled.

"You long-haired creep," she sobbed.

"Why, I'll..." He made as if to slap her, but couldn't as the plasterboard wall of the dressing room caved in and a wave of brawling bodies broke across the floor. My skinhead pals from LA were on the crest, working over a quartet of bearded guys.

They went for Strat as soon as they caught sight of his Eagles-esque mane. He grabbed Wanda and fled through the backdoor.

Skinhead Number One tossed me a set of car keys.

"Bring the car around to the back!" he yelled. "We're getting outa here!"

I snatched my gun off the floor and looked for the two punks. Too late. They were out the door and running across the parking lot. I bolted after them, but they were in a '54 Chevy and racing after Strat's '63 Corvette. *Screw the skinheads*, I thought, and climbed into their black Dodge Charger. A patch of smoking rubber was all I left behind.

On the freeway, it was like the Indy 500. Strat and Wanda had the early lead until Long Beach. Then the two punks pulled alongside and tried to elbow the Corvette off the road. Strat dodged behind an eighteen-wheeler and kept it between them. By Torrance the Chevy was sucking wind. Rodney was spinning Public Image Ltd over the airwaves, the perfect soundtrack for a hundred-mile-an-hour car chase up the Pacific coast. I kept the two cars in my sights and kept humping the accelerator.

Strat was heading for LA, that was sure. The punks seemed more worried about Wanda than about my nabbing them for Mitchell's murder. And what got me tangled up was Wanda's reaction to Strat. No cartwheels. Just the opposite. According to him they were sweethearts, except that Mitch Mitchell kept them apart to save her singing career. Maybe Belinda and her Go-Go crowd were right. Maybe I didn't understand Los Angeles. Or maybe I was spending too much time in too many cars on too many goddamned freeways.

Strat had definite plans. When he got to the city, he hopped off the freeway. On Olympic, he tried to shake us as he headed west. The first red light he jumped was a big mistake. A passing patrol car did a U-turn and joined the race.

The Corvette screeched around the corner at Highland. He peeled north toward Hollywood. By the time he reached Franklin, he had three cop cars on his tail, plus the punks, plus me. Traffic from the Hollywood Bowl was all backed up. Strat put his wheels on the sidewalk and shot westward.

I guessed he was heading for the canyons. He was going to try to lose us on the roads that corkscrew back into the Hollywood Hills. Once up there, a good driver like Strat could twist and turn faster than an Eric Clapton solo. He had musician buddies in Laurel Canyon that could hide him and his 'ludes for years.

Taking a sudden right off Franklin, he swerved onto a steep, narrow drive. Halfway up he must have realized the error. But with five cars coming up after him, there was no turning back. The road curved higher, around and around and around and came out in a parking lot for a Japanese restaurant with a great view and lousy food. Dead end.

Strat jerked to a halt, bowling over a couple of valets in monkey suits. He yanked Wanda from the car and made for the trees. The punks tried to follow; the LAPD cars corralled them. The cop on my tail thought he had me, too. I gunned the motor, aimed the Charger toward Tokyo, and bailed out into a sweet-smelling bush. The cop car kamikazeed the Charger, turning it into a flaming scrap heap.

Imitation oriental gardens surrounded the restaurant. It was a maze of gravel paths, lily ponds, hedgerows, and ornamental fakery. The gardens were planted to the very edge of the hill. After that was nothing. Sheer cliffs dropped all the way down to where the city lights rippled and shone.

I crouched in the shadows of a night-blooming hibiscus. The cops fanned out. A megaphone announced somebody needed to come out with his hands in the air. I moved farther down, keeping my head low. A fake plaster Zen temple stood at the edge where the gardens ended. A movement in the shrubs caught my eye. I waited. Drew my heater and waited. Wait long enough and everything comes your way.

Strat crawled out of the leaves. He had Wanda by the arm, gun to her head. They clambered into the Zen temple. I watched as he checked out his chances on the cliffside. It was his only way out.

"Forget it," I said, stepping out of the shadows. "You'll never make it alive."

He pulled the girl up on the temple's low wall, keeping his pistol to her skull.

"Butt out," he said. "I got no hassle with you."

"If you give up now, Strat, you'll get off with a couple of parking tickets."

"Don't come any closer! Or I'll blow her punk head off," he snarled, "just like I blew away Mitchell."

"You? But..."

"That's right. I killed Mitchell. He was the worst manger on the scene. A lot of musicians hated him. But I hated him worse than anybody. Wanna know why? Because he was gonna sign me up. Big record contact and everything. But then he had to go *punk*."

Strat spit the word out like it was dog piss.

"That morning in his office, he told me I was through. He said guys like me with long hair and laid-back music were passé. Instead, he was gonna give that contract to a new waver, a punk group name of Wanda and the Whips. I was so mad I blasted the guy on the spot. I swore I'd get even with these punks. And now..."

Now he was going to give Wanda a permanent chill.

"There he is!" a cop yelled. Searchlights flicked on. Strat growled.

"Don't shoot!" I shouted. "You'll hit the girl!"

Strat pointed his gun in the direction of the lights. The shots zinged through the cool night air. His balance was thrown off. The wall of the Zen temple gave way. He clutched at Wanda but I caught her as he fell. Strat gave out a miserable cry, then took the short, fatal way back to Hollywood, the city of dreams.

Lieutenant Keeler put his hand on my shoulder. "I heard all that," he said. "I guess you're in the clear, Ford."

Cops make me sick.

But Keeler did do me a favor.

The two punks from Costa Mesa were manacled in the back of the patrol car. He put the squeeze on them to tell me why they'd conked me on the head and kidnapped Wanda.

Turned out that the three of them were really Freda and the Frantics, famous in the South Bay towns as a hard-core punk band. Then Mitch Mitchell came along, promised Freda he'd make her a star. Broke up the act. It pissed off the two Frantics when they saw Mitchell selling Freda/Wanda as a rockabilly queen when her real scene was singing no-wave surf-punk. So they simply stole her back.

Why had I seem them running out of Mitchell's office the morning he was murdered?

"We went there to make him rip up Freda's contract," said one.

Strat had been there first, of course. That tied up the last loose thread, except for one. I looked around for Wanda. Or Freda. I found her in the back of the patrol car. The radio was tuned to Rodney's show, *Rodney on the KROQ*. The little blonde punk was snapping her fingers to D-Day and singing along to "Too Young to Date."

It was time for me to head back to the Big Apple.

The Backstory

THE FORD FAIRLANE STORIES first came to public attention through their publication in two quirky periodicals, *The New York Rocker* and the *LA Weekly*. The former focused on contemporary music and the latter was an "alternative weekly" devoted to local happenings. Neither had ever published fiction before, and the editorial decision to present stories about a "New Wave Private Eye" serialized in regular installments was not a likely bet.

The late nineteenth century was the heyday of serialized fiction, with Charles Dickens, Sir Arthur Conan Doyle, Alexandre Dumas, Henry James, and Herman Melville among its most popular practitioners. Harriet Beecher Stowe published *Uncle Tom's Cabin* in forty installments. More recently, Armistead Maupin's *Tales of the City* ran in San Francisco newspapers, and Tom Wolfe's *Bonfire of the Vanities* appeared in twenty-seven issues of *Rolling Stone.*

The premise, of course, is that the immediacy of the writing captures a contemporary sensibility that strikes a chord; avid readers hooked by cliffhangers at the end of each episode, rush to buy the publication to find out what happens next.

There was little evidence in the late 1970s, however, that punk rockers were avid readers, although several performers of the genre, such as Richard Hell, Jim Carroll, and Patti Smith, were active poets and writers. Recent books memorializing the era include Smith's *Just Kids*, Kim Gordon's *Girl in a Band*, and *Please Kill Me: An Uncensored Oral History of Punk* by Legs McNeil and Gillian McCain. But for the motley crowds crushed into CBGB or slamming the mosh pit at the Starwood, contemporary fiction was not necessarily a big draw.

Within this context, editors Andy Schwartz of *New York Rocker* and Jay Levin of *LA Weekly*— passionate about their publications, and with a particular editorial outlook attuned to their times— helped launch *The Adventures of Ford Fairlane*.

Similarly, but with a different object, filmmaker Floyd Mutrux got hold of the stories and became a Ford Fairlane fan, devoting nearly two years of his life to making a feature-length motion picture based on Rex Weiner's concept of a private eye who worked in the music business.

For the first time, in interviews by author and musicologist Pat Thomas, Schwartz, Levin, and Mutrux talk about why they took a chance on Ford Fairlane.

Interview with Andy Schwartz

IN APRIL 1980, THE *New York Rocker* launched *The Adventures of Ford Fairlane, New Wave Private Eye* as a six-part serialized story. Andy Schwartz was the editor and publisher of the monthly, tabloid-sized paper, which had a circulation of about twenty thousand and offices a short walk from the loft where Rex Weiner lived in what was then the warehouse district of Chelsea on Manhattan's west side.

A New York native, Andy Schwartz began writing about pop music in 1972 as an undergraduate at the University of Minnesota, and later wrote a weekly music column for the alternative weekly *Metropolis*. He also worked behind the counter of the legendary Minneapolis record shop Oar Folkjokeopus. Soon after returning to New York in 1977, Andy became publisher and editor of *New York Rocker*, the punk/new wave magazine founded by the late Alan Betrock. Under Schwartz's direction, *NYR* published forty-four issues and became one of the most widely read and influential American music publications. He became director of editorial services for Epic Records, a division of Sony Music, and has served as editor of the program book published for the Rock & Roll Hall off Fame's annual induction dinner. His recent clients include Time Life music and top-tier NYC jazz club, Jazz Standard.

The *New York Rocker* didn't normally print this kind of stuff, what inspired you to run the Ford Fairlane serial?

Schwartz: Because we hadn't printed that kind of thing before. No one had even tried to submit such a thing.

Do you remember what kind of reaction you were getting from readers?

Schwartz: No. I don't remember getting any particular correspondence or anything. Of course, this is like thirty-five years ago, so. But I thought it was an interesting and unique idea. It seemed to relate to the New York scene of the time, the club scene, and so on, so I just went with it. I can tell you it wasn't a big financial outlay on the part of the magazine.

What was your reaction when it was relayed into a movie? Were you surprised by that?

Schwartz: Well, yeah, because this was a period of almost a decade—like almost eight or nine years— between the time it ran as a serial in the magazine and the movie hit the screen. So, yeah, I was surprised.

Did you wind up seeing the movie?

Schwartz: No, I never have.

What would you say characterized the 1970s as a creative era?

Schwartz: Well, you know, it's a big question. Musically—I'll just speak to that—clearly the original punk rock movement, most of which was not even punk rock in the way that most people think of it. In other words, The Ramones are a template, or an archetype, but these other bands that were their contemporaries in New York—Blondie, Television, Patti Smith Group, Talking Heads—each one was a different idea, and few, if any, sounded like people's idea of punk rock. In that sense, the American creative impulse was moving in a bunch of different directions that were really, if they had anything in common, it was really only in response to the rock/pop mainstream of the period. If you look at the Hot 100 of 1978 it's like the softest, weakest, most gutless Hot 100 ever, you know? It's a ton of Bee Gees–related records, some of which were good pop records in and of themselves, but a lot of it is like Clapton to Neil Diamond, Elton John...all this soft rock from this period in 1978. So, what these bands that I'm talking about, the foundation of that scene—what they had in common was what they stood in opposition to.

And in the time of "Ford Fairlane," rent was still cheap, right?

Schwartz: That was certainly true. New York City was still very much like the New York City of lore. High crime, housing stock in decay, buildings abandoned by their landlords in places like the East Village and taken over by squatters. It was rough and tough. All of those elements that are now used to set the scene in movies and TV series about the city in the seventies was quite real, which is not to say that there weren't a great number of wealthy people living in New York and major corporations doing business everyday, you know. But the seventies was when the music business, in large part, moved from New York to Los Angeles. Capitol had always been based in LA, but Jac Holzman's Elektra label was moved to LA under him and then under different CEOs until it was moved back to New York. Warner Bros. had always been based in Burbank. Columbia Records had been, as a part of CBS, based in New York, but established a major headquarters and a much stronger presence in Los Angeles in this period, and so on. There was considerable movement. RCA was headquartered in LA.

Can you tie the Ford Fairlane stories to any other writing from that era or genre? If someone asked you what the stories were like, and they hadn't read them yet, would you be able to give a comparison to anything?

Schwartz: It seems to me that in this period of the late seventies and into the eighties there was something of a revival of interest in classic, hardboiled literature. Even the discovery of authors whose work had been completely classified as drugstore exploitation books, someone like Charles Willeford, Jim Thompson, people like that, I think underwent a kind of rediscovery, beginning in this period. Some of those books were reprinted. As far as Rex's contemporaries, I'm not sure really who would come to mind here. I was pretty busy publishing a magazine; I didn't necessarily keep up with current literary events of the time, you know? So, this is why I have a hard time thinking a suitable comparison to the Ford Fairlane stories. This era seems to be making a comeback in terms of a whole slew of memoirs. Richard Hell did a book about two years ago, Robert Lloyd just did a book, Patti Smith's done two volumes. Richard Boch did a book on the Mudd Club.

Why would somebody who hasn't read the Ford Fairlane stories before be interested in them—what would you tell a younger person is the attraction?

Schwartz: I'd tell them it was fun to read and that it tells an intriguing, fictional story set in that time and place, and it's got a degree of verisimilitude with real musicians and real people weaving in and out of the scene. It's just a fun thing to read.

Interview by Pat Thomas

Interview with Jay Levin

IN THE FALL OF 1980, just as the concluding episode of the first "Ford Fairlane" story was published in the *New York Rocker*, a new "adventure" was launched in Los Angeles. Episode One of *The Adventures of Ford Fairlane, New Wave Private Eye* appeared on September 12, 1980 in the *LA Weekly*, kicking off a six-part serial in the same way as the *New York Rocker*, but a distinct departure from the weekly's usual editorial mix of crusading local journalism and hipster entertainment reviews.

Jay Levin is the founder and former CEO and editor-in-chief of the award-winning *LA Weekly* newspaper, which he sold in 1996 and went on to run three other media companies and start three nonprofits. Currently, he is president of the Big EQ Campaign, an educational advocacy group. Levin is also a life and executive coach.

What inspired you to publish the Ford Fairlane serial? Something that the *LA Weekly* typically didn't do.

Jay Levin: We were very experimental and open-minded about what would work and what wouldn't work. We didn't want to be too predictable, so if something came along that I really liked or that I thought would speak to an audience but would be in the gestalt of the audience—well, that was an operational theme we had at the time. I came out of New York, I got on the phone with Rex about his stories—at that time it was running in the *New York Rocker*. He talked about merging it to LA and I thought, "OK, this would be fun and an easy read," and, "Why not?" I'd once asked Charles Bukowski to do a column and he said, "Yeah, as long as I get to write whatever I want." I said, "Yeah." So, he did three or four and they were fun and fine—Bukowski kind of stuff—and then he did one where he had this mother take a girl to an eye doctor and the eye doctor closes the door, says the mother can't come in, and wants to molest and scare the little girl into sex acts by showing her a bottle of eyes, and he's saying, "I'm gonna put your eyes in here unless you cooperate with me." He expected me to run it! And I thought, "Well, this guy's just testing me. He's gotta just be testing me." I said, I'm not running it, so he quit. [*Laughs*] I knew that with Rex that wouldn't happen. I thought what he was doing was fun and cheeky. It was not a hard decision.

This is sort of the golden era of the entertainment weeklies, right?

Levin: Yeah, this was sort of in the middle of the golden era. It got more golden for the weekly over the next twenty-five years.

Around that time period, when the Ford Fairlane stories ran, rents were still cheap in New York, which allowed artists and musicians to do their thing in a loft that they probably paid a hundred dollars a month for. Was LA similar back then?

Levin: Yeah, there was that scene there, for sure. LA also created the wise-guy cop writers, the LA writers like Raymond Chandler, so Rex's story sort of caught a bit of that flavor as well.

Do you remember any feedback from the readers?

Levin: I don't remember anything negative. People either liked it, thought it was relevant. Overall, my memory of it was that we had a positive response to it.

Were you surprised that a decade later it became a movie?

Levin: No, and hooray for Rex. I knew that was his goal, but I thought it was a long shot. It was popular and I think it helped him get the movie deal so that was great.

Did you see the movie?

Levin: I can't remember. [*Laughs*] I don't remember a lot of what happened back in those years.

Interview by Pat Thomas

Interview with Floyd Mutrux

NOT LONG AFTER *THE Adventures of Ford Fairlane, New Wave Private Eye* ran in the *LA Weekly* in the fall of 1980, the stories came to the attention of LA-based writer/producer/director Floyd Mutrux. By October 1981, he and Rex Weiner were developing a screenplay for a motion picture version under contract at Columbia Pictures, to be directed by Mutrux. It never went into production. Not until the stories were optioned, developed into a screenplay by a series of writers, and later produced in 1990 by Joel Silver at 20th Century Fox, and directed by Renny Harlin, did the stories become an actual major studio motion picture. But Ford Fairlane was first introduced to Hollywood as a viable movie project through Mutrux.

Floyd Mutrux grew up in Houston and Los Angeles. After a stint with Second City in Chicago and New York, he attended Columbia University before returning to LA in the 1970s. He wrote and directed a documentary for Warner Bros. about heroin on the LA streets called *Dusty and Sweets McGee*, which earned rave reviews. Mutrux went on to write and produce the action comedy *Freebie and the Bean* at Warner Bros., one of the biggest grossing films of 1974; the next year he directed *Aloha, Bobby and Rose*, released by Columbia, the sixth largest grossing picture of the year. Among many movies he was involved in, Floyd directed *American Hot Wax* at Paramount, about Alan Freed, the 1950s radio DJ and concert promoter who coined the term "rock 'n' roll." Today, Mutrux is the writer of Broadway hit musicals *Million Dollar Quarter* and *Baby It's You.*

When Rex Weiner met Mutrux, the veteran Hollywood filmmaker had recently completed writing and directing *Hollywood Knights*— starring Tony Danza and a young Michelle Pfeiffer—a summertime teen comedy, which grossed $10 million on a budget of $2.5 million for Columbia Pictures. Mutrux seemed to be on a roll.

How did the Ford Fairlane stories first come to your attention?

Mutrux: A guy named Neil Silver worked for me. He had worked for the record producer Lou Adler. Lou and I had produced the Cheech & Chong movie *Up in Smoke*. Neil read it somewhere. I don't remember where. He spoke to me about it.

What interested you about the stories?

Mutrux: I'd had it in my mind at some point to do some kind of Dashiell Hammett, *Farewell,*

My Lovely kind of story—the PI, the girl, whatever. I had an idea to do one of those. Like the series James Garner was in that ran for many years about this kind of guy—he lived in a trailer out on the beach, a detective who doesn't carry a gun and has an assistant who's an idiot.

I'd done a ton of cop movies, maybe ten different pilots for TV, and the movie *Freebie and the Bean*. I hung around cops a lot in the parking lot of the Whisky a Go Go. The Sunset Strip belonged to the Sheriff's Department. There was one cop, a big tough guy, heart of gold—but you hoped he'd better not be the bad guy—a big Mexican American who worked homicide. He was at the Whisky a lot. It was kind of a mobbed-up joint; Jimmy Hoffa was arrested there. A lot of wise guys hanging there, gangsters, whatever. That part of the Strip was what it was.

Along the way I decided to write about this PI who had a lot of history that was cloudy. What was the music called at that time, The Pretenders, Soft Cell, Pet Shop Boys—new wave? I wrote about a new wave detective, a guy who drove around town in a Rent-a-Wreck and as a policy didn't do cases involving runaways. On the door it says, "No Runaways." Of course, the first case he gets into ultimately involves a runaway. And his whole history is revealed—the girl that he loved, the woman on the Strip that got away, the one he always thought was dead. The runaway turns out to be his illegitimate daughter that he didn't know about, and her mother is the woman he'd been in love with. The story was called *The Girl With The Purple Hair*. The girl's name was Tomorrow. The sequel was going to be called *Kiss Tomorrow Goodbye*. That was in my mind.

So you optioned Rex Weiner's stories and...

Mutrux: Rex did a series of articles. I don't know that I read them all. What happened was, I told Columbia what I was doing on [a project about the Hillside Strangler called] *The Strangler*, and I was working also on the prequel—or was it the sequel?—to *Up in Smoke*. Barry Diller didn't want to do the original movie. We were doing *American Me*, and at one point Al Pacino was doing it. But he chose not to drink and took the year off from work. That's what his analyst suggested. So I was in the middle of it. Al and I were drinking together. We were doing rewrites on a movie called *Scarecrow* with Gene Hackman, won Best Picture at Cannes. We were hanging out, drinking at Dan Tana's, the Troubadour, and all that. Then Al agreed to do *Bobby Deerfield* about a sports car driver. I was going to teach Al how to drive a stick shift while we were drinking, you can imagine how that worked out.

Anyway, this was somewhere between *American Hot Wax* and a great script I'd done called *Happy Hour*, Jon Voight was on board. It kept starting and stopping. Studios changed, executives changed.

I'd also written a very strong script about the Hillside Strangler, a famous case where a number of women were snatched, they disappeared, their nude bodies were always discovered on a hillside. The script never got made. Neither did *Happy Hour*.

It was in the middle of all those things that I decided I wanted to try to do the *Girl with the Purple Hair*. I contacted Rex. Frank Price was head of Columbia Pictures, the studio where I was doing the Hillside Strangler. I said to Frank I wanted to do this other thing. At that time they would do anything I wanted. *Aloha, Bobby And Rose* and *Freebie and the Bean* had made a lot of money.

I described to Frank what I liked about Ford Fairlane. New wave music, the music that came after rock and roll went away. First there was rock and roll, then there was Michael Jackson, then it was gone. MTV told you everything you wanted to know. Music used to be a hip thing. Everyone who was into rock and roll, you know—it was like a secret club until it got out to the public. MTV killed all that. The bands stopped touring. They just did MTV, and guess what? When a band's on the road—that's when they write. They'd go on tour for six months and come back with an album. What do you think Mick and Keith do when they're on the road? They take a barroom queen from Memphis down to the French Quarter in New Orleans, get wasted, and they write about it. "Get Yer Ya-Ya's Out!" The Eagles went out on the road, they set up in a hotel, and they couldn't leave, you know? MTV fucked it up. The bands never had a chance to grow. MTV and the record companies killed the music. It was over.

So how did Ford Fairlane fit into this?

Mutrux: All of the movies I've done have been scored with an AM car radio. That process was always in my mind when I'd write a movie that I was going to direct. For me the music was part of my lifestyle. Ford Fairlane fit into that mode for me, in telling this kind of romantic story of a PI with a dark backstory. So I said to Rex, okay— so write the story. We hung around a bit, places like the China Club, a kind of a decadent period in LA, a lot of celebrities, everyone was doing a little cocaine, maybe a little too much cocaine. There was a lost weekend I remember... Listen, everybody from Harry Nilsson to Rod Stewart...it was a different life then, that's all. Well, that was the eighties. My best friend was Richard Perry, the record producer. Still is. He had a house in the hills. You walked in—John Lennon, they were all there.

Why didn't Ford Fairlane get made at Columbia?

Mutrux: Rex worked on a draft of the script. Columbia put it in turnaround. A producer I'd worked with, Sidney Beckerman [*Portnoy's Complaint, Marathon Man, Marlowe, Red Dawn,* and *The Sicilian*], well, he came in and we ended up changing studios to Embassy Pictures. I was going to direct and I was going to do it with Mel Gibson. Or Mickey Rourke. Rex would not be involved. I started to write about this new wave detective who lived above a nude bar in Chinatown, drove a Rent-a-Wreck, and the Girl with the Purple Hair. But when it came time to pull the trigger, the studio owner, Jerry Perenchio, sold Embassy. Took his money and bought four or five Spanish radio stations. The movie went into turnaround again. I walked away. At that point, Ford Fairlane went back to Rex.

Did you see the movie, *The Adventures of Ford Fairlane*, that 20th Century Fox ultimately made?

Mutrux: Didn't see the film, didn't read the script. Andrew Dice Clay was the opposite of Mel Gibson or Mickey Rourke. My Ford Fairlane was a real guy. I was doing my own thing with that character. If somebody doesn't want to do my thing, that's okay.

Interview by Pat Thomas

About Rex Weiner

COFOUNDER AND PUBLISHER OF the pioneering *New York Ace* newspaper (1971–73) and, according to his FBI file, an ant-war activist and founding member of the editorial staff of *High Times* magazine, Weiner's articles have appeared in, *Vanity Fair, Los Angeles Times Sunday Magazine, The New Yorker, New York Observer,* and *LA Weekly* as well as *Rolling Stone Italia* and *L'Officiel Hommes*. A native of Brooklyn, his last New York publishing job was editor of *Swank* ("The Magazine for Men") before moving west to Los Angeles. In addition to *The Adventures of Ford Fairlane,* Rex Weiner's produced screenwriting credits include *Forgotten Prisoners, The Amnesty Files,* one of TNT's first made-for-TV movies. He was one of the first writers brought on board to launch the TV series *Miami Vice.*

Weiner ruined morning coffee for many entertainment industry executives as a *Daily Variety* staff reporter from 1993–1997. With Deanne Stillman, Weiner coauthored *The Woodstock Census* (Viking), a widely hailed survey of the sixties generation's impact on American society.

He has written about LA politics and culture as West Coast correspondent for the *Forward*, and is an investigative reporter for *Capital and Main*. He lives in Los Angeles where he serves on the board of Beyond Baroque, the literary center, and in Todos Santos, Baja California Sur, Mexico where he is a cofounder and director of the Todos Santos Writers Workshop.

Acknowledgments

THANKS TO PAT THOMAS, author of *Listen, Whitey!* and *Did It! Jerry Rubin, An American Revolutionary*, for interviewing Jay Levin, Andy Schwartz, and Floyd Mutrux, and thanks to those guys for cooperating, as well as being Ford Fairlane's willing accomplices in the first place. Many thanks to Tyson Cornell and the Rare Bird team for their diligent work and expertise. I am grateful to Deanne Stillman for the use of her photo on the cover (yes, that's me when I was writing and living these stories), and to my attorney Linda Lichter for safeguarding my work. A salute to my friends John Densmore and Jonathan Shaw for being early readers. My gratitude, always, to my companion author Jeanne McCulloch for her encouragement and support. And to all my amigos at the Todos Santos Writers Workshop—muchas gracias!

—Rex Weiner